Sir William Muir

The Honourable James Thomason

Lieutenant-Governor N.-W. P., India, 1843-1853 A.D

Sir William Muir

The Honourable James Thomason
Lieutenant-Governor N.-W. P., India, 1843-1853 A.D

ISBN/EAN: 9783337189686

Printed in Europe, USA, Canada, Australia, Japan

Cover: Foto ©Raphael Reischuk / pixelio.de

More available books at **www.hansebooks.com**

THE HONOURABLE
JAMES THOMASON

LIEUTENANT-GOVERNOR
N.-W. P., INDIA

1843–1853 A.D.

BY

Sir WILLIAM MUIR

K.C.S.I., LL.D., D.C.L., PH.D.

[CALCUTTA REVIEW, 1853.]

1. *Directions for Revenue Officers in the North-Western Provinces.*
2. *Calcutta Gazette Extraordinary, October* 3, 1853.
3. *A Sermon preached in St. Paul's Church, Agra, on occasion of the death of the Honourable James Thomason, by the Rev. T. V. French, M.A., Church Missionary in Agra.*

EDINBURGH
T. & T. CLARK, 38 GEORGE STREET
1897

CONTENTS

PREFACE

—◆—

MR. THOMASON was appointed Lieutenant-Governor of the North-Western Provinces of India in 1843, and administered that Government till his death in 1853. The following account was published in the *Calcutta Review* shortly after, with a view to lay before the public the history of a great and good Administrator. And now, though after two-score years, it may still be of interest, not only for the noble example it gives to our Indian authorities, but also as tracing the origin of Institutions that owe their birth to Thomason.

As Secretary to the Agra Government during the last two years of Mr. Thomason's life, I had the special opportunity of close and confidential intercourse with him both in public and private, in camp as well as in his Agra home. It also chanced that several years before, when Magistrate of Futtehpore, I had the privilege of attending upon him as he marched through that District, and thus of learning his wise and kindly attitude towards the officials and people about him in these his yearly tours. In my diary of the day I find warm mention of the gracious treatment of my family and myself on that

occasion in the following passage, which I may quote
as illustrative of his camp life :—

"He was very attentive, and came to see us kindly every evening.
On both Sundays he had public worship, when he read the prayers
and an excellent sermon. I used to ride with him half the stage, and
then mounting with him on his howda the other half. His conversation was very interesting. His views upon revenue matters
are so systematically arranged and so clearly developed that one
cannot converse with him without deriving great advantage."

He was so good as in 1847 to appoint me Secretary
of the Revenue Board at Agra ; and thus residing at his
Headquarters, I was able to see much of him. But
it was not till 1852 that I was brought into more
close connection with him as Secretary to the
Government over which he presided. During the
cold season of 1852–53 I accompanied him on his
tour through the Allahabad and Benares Provinces as
far as Goruckpore, and thus also through his old
district of Jounpore where he had first learned to
know the people and gain his village experience, and
where the memories of domestic happiness evidently
touched him to the quick. It was then that I
gained the intimate knowledge of his administration
which I have here endeavoured to commemorate.
During the summer of 1853 he fell into weakly
health, and purposed in the autumn to profit by
the bracing air of Nynee Tal. On his journey he was
spending a few days with his daughter at Bareilly,
when his illness took a fatal turn, and I received
the sad intelligence of his death on my way to
meet him. Returning to Agra, it was one of my

earliest endeavours, with his administration still fresh in mind, to write the brief outline of it, which I now republish.

A few years ago Sir Richard Temple published a biography of Mr. Thomason, and admirably has he — discharged the task.[1] But his object was to write the life at large, rather than enter into the details of the North-Western Provinces administration, as I have here endeavoured. His book therefore in no way supersedes the present review, which I submit for the acceptance of those interested in the government of India.

The lesson it teaches is one for all engaged in any kind of administrative work; and for India, in that respect it is unique. It leads all round. How ceaseless was Thomason in studying the needs of the country, searching out its wants and means of improvement at every step, and perfecting all parts of his administration. How beautiful his intercourse with the people. How instructive, as well for himself as for the officers around him, the counsels he ever took with them, whether on tour or in his home at Agra. To this day we see the fruits of his wise directions. Witness the scheme of Village schools; the Roorkee workshops and the College which so aptly bears his name,—a school of technical training for all India; and chiefest of all, the Ganges Canal itself,—which, but for him becoming a mere boat canal, has proved the grandest work of irrigation the world has ever seen.

[1] *James Thomason*, by Sir Richard Temple. Oxford : The Clarendon Press, 1893.

Examples these of the fertility of his genius bearing fruit for the nation as the years roll on.

To show the feeling evoked by the death of Thomason, I may embody in this Preface two passages by writers well acquainted with him. In the review of Lord Dalhousie's administration, written the year following his death, we read :—

"We have hitherto omitted all direct mention of one of the most distressing events of the past year ; we allude of course to the death of James Thomason, the honoured ruler of the North-Western Provinces. This event . . . threw a gloom over the close of 1853. We have lately had occasion to present in this *Review* a notice of the late Lieut.-Governor's character and distinguished career ; and the time is hardly yet come when those who loved his example in life can talk of him with tongues that do not falter and eyes that do not fill. For his nomination to the Government of Agra, we hold that the country is under a debt to Lord Ellenborough, which may be a set-off to the song of Somnath and to other eccentricities. The late Lieut.-Governor had been nearly ten years in office. . . . He died on the scene of his labours amidst a people which he had benefited, with some beloved relatives not absent from his dying couch ; and happy is the man, we would say with all the solemnity that such a subject demands, who crowns a life of such ability by such a Christian death."[1]

Again, the same year, in a review of the *Directions to Revenue Officers*, there is the following passage by another writer which I may quote in full :—

"The volume which we have placed at the head of this paper is one, but *only one*, of the legacies left by its gifted author to these Provinces, for which he lived and died ; and in detailing the duties of a Collector of Revenue, surely some notice of him who has taught by his words these duties, is not out of place.

"When, in 1843, the post of Lieutenant-Governor fell unexpectedly vacant, and the most fastidious of Governor-Generals, who possessed the divining-rod of ability, and whose appointments were marked by a wondrous prescience,—looked round for a person fit to hold the reins at that crisis, the Foreign Secretary stood alone, the most distin-

---

guished of his contemporaries. He may not have had the political skill and vigour which characterised Hastings and Elphinstone ; . . . not so great in public enthusiasm as Metcalfe, but in something greater ; not so popular as Clerk, but more deserving to be loved ; he has left us better than the frothy declamations of Napier, the songs of triumph of Ellenborough, or the carnage-bought victories of Gough. All around him was war, but he calmly worked out his schemes of improvement, and showed that peace has her victories no less re-nowned than those of war.

"Some achieve greatness ; he was both good and great, an example to the servants of Government, that great ability can be united to purity and religion, that success in this world need not steel the heart to the concerns of the next. To enumerate his actions would be to notice every improvement for the last ten years in these Provinces, for he could combine wisdom and sound views with the most intimate detail. Amidst the glitter and tinsel of the modern great, it was grateful to find something solid to rest on. He was greater because untitled, and because undecorated he appears the more distinguished ; — . . . and when the question of the government of a great Dependency was agitated in the Senate, his actions alone obtained universal praise ; his administration alone stood the test of inquiry.

"In the midst of the applause he died. Ere the last echo of praise had reached us, while a new proconsular wreath was weaving for his honoured head, while another lustrum of usefulness and advantage was opening out to him, to be followed, with God's blessing, by years of happiness in his native land, he passed away. It was not to be ; . . . he was snatched away by one of those unaccountable dispensa-tions, to which we can only bow in silence, and believe that the mission entrusted to him had been accomplished. And so sudden was his death, that the functions of government for a time stood suspended, the good ship started from her track as the rudder fell suddenly from the hand of the experienced steersman.

"Let no masses of stone, or useless mausoleum, be raised to com-memorate so good and simple-minded a man ; let the testimonial be, like his own character, practical, unostentatious, and beneficent to the people whom he loved so well. It may do for lordlings to be recorded on kindred blocks of unprofitable masonry, by the pre-sumptuous column, or the unmeaning obelisk. Let this man live among us, as lives a worthy rival in a sister Presidency. Let us learn to connect the moral improvement of the people with the names of Elphinstone and Thomason."[1]

---

[1] *Calcutta Review*, Vol. XXIII. p. 160. Article V., *Directions to Revenue Officers*, by James Thomason, Lieut.-Governor, Nov. 1, 1849.

In his biography of Thomason, Sir Richard Temple was good enough to quote the passage from my review, in which I sum up my estimate of Thomason's character;[1] and then he adds the following passage from a letter I had recently addressed to him on the subject:—

"Looking back after so long a period, Sir William now writes:—

"'When I wrote this description of Thomason in 1853, the close relation in which I had just lived with him as my Chief and guide of my life as his Secretary, might be supposed to have unduly magnified him in my eyes. Yet in the long interval that has since elapsed, and the large acquaintance I have had with Statesmen both in India and at home, I can truly say that my conception of his virtues and commanding position as a wise and illustrious Governor, as well as an exemplary Christian and faithful Friend, has only been heightened by the lapse of time, and that I regard him as the best of Rulers it has been my lot to be associated with.'"[2]

And with this I close what has been to me a labour of love, as well as a mark of dutiful regard for the memory of one to whom I look back as my early Friend and Guide.

W. M.

EDINBURGH, 1897.

[1] See below, p. 88.
[2] *James Thomason*, by Sir Richard Temple, p. 193.

THE

HONOURABLE JAMES THOMASON

Late Lieut.-Governor of the North-Western
Provinces of the Bengal Presidency

From the " Calcutta Review," 1853. Sixth Article.

1. *Directions for Revenue Officers in the North-Western Provinces of the Bengal Presidency, regarding the Settlement and Collection of the Land Revenue, and the other duties connected therewith.* Promulgated under the authority of the Honourable the Lieutenant-Governor. Agra, November 1, 1849. Second edition, Calcutta, 1850.

2. *Calcutta Gazette Extraordinary,* October 3, 1853 (on Mr. Thomason's death).

3. *A Sermon preached in St. Paul's Church, Agra, on occasion of the death of the Honourable James Thomason, Lieutenant-Governor of the North-Western Provinces.* By the Rev. T. V. French, M.A., late Fellow of University College, Oxford, and Church Missionary in Agra. October 2, A.D. MDCCCLIII. Published at the request of the Churchwardens of St. Paul's, and of other friends. Agra.

A GREAT MAN has passed from among us—a man ennobled, not by any one act of transcendent genius, or feat of moral daring, but by the far rarer merit of a long series of distinguished actions, all successfully

15

bearing upon the happiness and well-being of millions of our species. Such an one was JAMES THOMASON, the late Lieutenant-Governor of the North-Western Provinces of the Bengal Presidency.

It is not our intention to give an elaborate biographical notice of the deceased Statesman, or to attempt to assign his place in the history of India. The scene of his life is but close and recent; it admits not of the mellowed tints imparted by distance; and without these, the lineaments of biography are too sharp to be attractive, too brightly coloured to secure the verdict of impartiality. Still, as Reviewers of all that concerns the welfare of India, we cannot decline the task of briefly tracing the progress of Mr. Thomason's career, and presenting a hasty sketch of the administration by which he has achieved a name second to none in the array of India's Civil Governors.

James Thomason was born at Shelford, in the vicinity of Cambridge, on the 3rd of May 1804; but he was yet in early childhood when his father, the Rev. T. Thomason, relinquished the parochial charge of that delightful spot, and devoted himself to ministerial labour in India. Towards the close of 1808 he arrived in India with his family, but not before he had experienced, at the Sandheads, the fearful perils of shipwreck. The *Travers* went to pieces on a reef within sight of land, and Mr. Thomason, with his wife and children, half-naked, drenched and affrighted, escaped with difficulty and danger, in the ship's boats to the *Earl of Spencer*, which providentially was near at hand.[1]

The remainder of James Thomason's childhood was passed with his parents in Calcutta. In 1814, at the age of ten, he was sent to England. There he was fortunate in being welcomed with all the warmth of a parent, by the great and good Mr. Simeon, who had been the constant friend and frequent guest of his father and mother at Shelford. The eager affection with which he received his youthful charge makes us love all the more the venerable Simeon, though one smiles at his almost maternal care and inexperienced anxiety. He assures his father that "flannels will be ready to put on at a moment," and communicates to his mother the alarm he felt at finding him one day out fishing. The sober conclusion to which he comes, that *even after this* he did not repent his charge, is characteristic and amusing :—

" Be assured that if I were indeed his father, I could not feel much more for him than I do. He was imprudently fishing by the riverside, without hat or coat or waistcoat. Hearing only that he was fishing with little James Farish, I went full of anxiety to find him ; and finding him in such a situation, it was almost a dagger to my heart. But no evil occurred. I began to feel how great a matter I had undertaken ; but I do not repent, and I trust I shall never give you cause to repent."—*Life*, p. 398.

It is curious to observe that the *inquiring nature* of his mind, which continued to be one of the distinctive characteristics of Mr. Thomason's later days, was that which at this early period first impressed Simeon.

[1] See the account of this event. —*Life of Thomason*, p. 142, and *Life of Simeon*, p. 260.

2

" In liveliness and sweetness of disposition," he writes
in his first letter, " and in tenderness of spirit, he far
exceeds my most sanguine expectations.   What was said
by ——— of his inquisitiveness (his *spirit of inquiry* I
mean) was delightfully verified all along the road. . . .
Many of his questions were such as a man, a traveller
of sound sense and judgment, would have asked, and led
to explanations which it was the delight of my heart
to give." [1]   And again, to his mother (though here the
first clause finds no correspondent feature in after life) :
" He is, as you say, a little idle ; but very sensible and
acute in his questions." [2]

Simeon shortly after put him to a private school at
Aspenden, twenty-two miles from Cambridge, where
he appears to have remained about four years.   At
the age of fourteen he was transferred for two or
three years to the care of Mr. (now Archdeacon)
Hodson, at Stansted.   In both seminaries he signalised
himself by gaining prizes.

In 1821, when sixteen or seventeen years of age,
he went to Haileybury College.   Here we have
another characteristic view of the simplicity of
Simeon's solicitude, in his anxious and solemn
remonstrance at the monthly college report being
on one occasion rendered as " regular and correct," instead of " *quite* regular and correct " ; the
difference turning out to be caused by the neglect
of some college formality of no consequence what-

---

[1] *Life of Simeon*, p. 394.   [2] *Idem*, p. 397.

ever.[1]   Mr. Thomason, in after life, used to relate the
incident with a smile.

At Haileybury he distinguished himself by most
exemplary assiduity, and carried off many prizes and
medals.[2]   In 1822 Simeon writes to his father : " On
the 23rd May I intend to go to see him receive his
last prizes ; and on the 1st of June, I hope, your
mother and I shall sail with him, as I did with you,
. . . as far as the pilot goes."[3]   On the 19th September he landed in India.   In June 1823 he was
reported qualified for the public service, but was
allowed to continue in the college to prosecute the
study of Mohammedan Law.   In December of the
same year we find him appointed Assistant Registrar
to the Sudder Court at Calcutta.   About the same
time Simeon writes to his father : " I delight to hear
such blessed tidings of my beloved James.   Give my
kindest love to him.   We bear him in sweet remembrance, and most affectionately long for his welfare in
every possible way."[4]

It was, indeed, one of the greatest privileges we can
imagine, to have been, in the season of youth, for eight
years under the immediate charge of the apostolical
Simeon.   His simplicity of character, and earnestness
of purpose, fitted him eminently to be an influential
guide, as well as an attractive pattern, for a young

---

[1] *Life of Simeon*, p. 556.
[2] Among the subjects for which prizes were awarded, the following
occur, some of them repeatedly :—*Mathematics, Political Economy,
Law, Classical Literature, History.*
[3] *Life of Simeon*, p. 562.   [4] *Idem*, p. 589.

man; while his cheerful temperament and buoyant spirits exhibited religion in the most inviting aspect. Whether owing to this influence or not, it is certain that James Thomason was, throughout his life, guided by the same depth of religious sentiment and the same catholicity of principle, as animated Simeon.

Mr. Thomason remained attached to the Sudder Court, as Assistant Registrar, till 1826, when we find him appointed to officiate as Judge of the Jungle Mehals. In the same year he submitted to an examination in the College of Fort William as to proficiency in Mohammedan Law, which he had been prosecuting more or less since he was reported qualified for service. The examiners pronounced the highest eulogium on the "intense application and extraordinary talent" brought by him to bear upon the subject ;[1] and the Government conferred upon him an honorary grant of 3000 rupees. In the following year, 13th February 1827, he was obliged, by severe indisposition, to seek a restoration of health in a

---

[1] The following is an extract from the *Calcutta Gazette* of 28th July 1826 :—

"From the studious habits and tried abilities of Mr. Thomason, we were led to expect the display of extraordinary attainments. We assigned, therefore, to that gentleman the performance of exercises proportionally arduous ; and it affords us sincere gratification to state that our estimate, high as it was, of his acquirements, fell short of the reality. When we say that the translations were made with the utmost fidelity, accuracy, and despatch, we bear but inadequate testimony to his merits. In the course of three or four hours, Mr. Thomason not only performed what was required of him, but he found leisure also to make judicious annotations on abstruse passages, thereby

voyage to England, where he joined his father then also on a temporary visit at home.

Within two years he returned to India, and in 1829 was reattached to the Sudder Court, as Deputy Registrar and Preparer of Reports. Shortly after we find him officiating as Judge and Magistrate of the suburbs of Calcutta, and Superintendent of the Allipore Jail. In 1830, he was appointed to act as Deputy Secretary to Government in the Territorial department; and in the beginning of 1831, permanently posted to the same office in the Judicial and Revenue departments. While thus in a position most favourable for gaining an insight into the general working of our Government, it may be gathered that his attention was first attracted to the subject of education, for we find him in the same year appointed a member of the General Committee of Public Instruction. He had also devoted himself laboriously to the mastery of the Hindoo, as well as the Mohammedan sources of law; and interleaved copies of *Menu* and of the *Hedaya*, with carefully recorded notes of difficult

furnishing satisfactory proof, that to the capacity of consulting original legal authorities, he has added a considerable knowledge of the law itself. Mr. Thomason read a passage of the *Hedaya* in the presence of the law officers of the Sudder Dawanny Adalut, to whom he explained the meaning in the Persian language, and who expressed themselves in the highest degree gratified by the learning and acumen which he displayed."

The report is signed by Macnaghten, Riddell, and Ousely; and in consequence of it, although the giving of honorary premia had been discontinued by order of the Court of Directors, yet, as it was shown that he had been at the study before the prohibition was made, he received the grant of Rs. 3000.

or curious points, attest the intelligence and the assiduity with which he pursued the study.[1] It is not often that we find a combined attention thus success-fully turned at once to Arabic and to Sanscrit literature.

But it is not in the Secretarial bureau alone, or in the private study, that administrative capacity is to be gained. It is not enough that the red tape be ever and anon untied, bundles of correspondence read and digested, and the busy pen daily employed in carefully expressed and nimbly recorded despatches. It is true that the views of enlightened officers, ably employed in active duty, may thus be thoroughly mastered, and valuable notes and memoranda may be multiplied till the Secretariat shelves groan beneath them. But no study will supply the place of *personal experience*; and so long as an officer has not himself mixed with the people, and come into immediate contact with them as their District Officer, his opinions cannot, properly speaking, be called *his own*, since they are grounded, not upon personal observation, but upon the reports and experience of others.

It was fortunate therefore for himself—more fortunate for the country at large—that Mr. Thomason did not long continue in Calcutta. On the 18th of September 1832, he was appointed Magistrate and Collector of Azimgurh, a large and populous

[1] These copies are now in the library of the College at Agra, to which he bequeathed the greater portion of his books.

district[1] in the Benares division, bordering upon Oudh.

The Vice-President in Council, Sir Charles Metcalfe, had been so impressed with "the marked ability and efficiency" of his official conduct (for during the absence of Mr. Macnaghten he appears to have had the sole charge of the Secretariat), that with the concurrence of Mr. Ross, he publicly communicated to him, on his departure, the cordial approbation and thanks of the Government.[2]

A small portion of his charge, comprised in one Pergunnah, had been permanently assessed on the principles of the Bengal settlement: the remainder stood upon the same unsettled basis as the rest of the North-Western Provinces. The Revenue Survey was about to be introduced into the district; preliminary to that, the boundaries of every village had to be defined, and disputes adjusted; then was to follow the Revenue Settlement and Record of Rights, framed under Regulations VII. of 1822 and IX. of 1833, on the principles laid down by the great and lamented Robert Merttins Bird. Here was a noble sphere for the acquisition of knowledge and experience; for devising expedients to facilitate the rapid and correct disposal of public business; and for examining how the series of Acts, which issue from the Council Board

---

[1] Azimgurh contains 2510 square miles, and has a population of 1,653,251 souls, so that the number of persons falls at the enormous rate of 657 to the square mile.

[2] Letter from Mr. J. R. Colvin, Deputy Secretary, dated 5th February 1833.

or the Governor, and of which the outer and upper features are often alone observable from the Secretariat chair, affect the people in the sober realities of every-day life,—when, through a variety of intervening media, they at last reach down into actual contact with them. Here, too, were golden opportunities for exercising command both upon the Native and European mind, and for testing the influence possessed over others in swaying their opinions and guiding their actions.

Upon all these objects, the busy mind of Thomason was ceaselessly engaged. Instructions were drawn up, with diligent thoughtfulness, for the guidance of his Covenanted assistants in the conduct of the independent charges assigned to each; and as the Settlement drew on, carefully framed rules for the adjustment of disputes and other matters, were laid down for his Tehseeldars and European staff. Upon these, he sought to elicit the suggestions and remarks of his head Assistants; such criticisms, both in writing and in personal conference, he was forward to invite and to take into ready consideration. But an opinion or rule once carefully arrived at, had always been the result of such mature and sound deliberation that, however much contested, it was rarely abandoned. The general interests of his charge engaged also his constant attention. We find him, for instance, objecting in his private capacity, to the Legislative Council against a proposed enactment for investing the Magistrate with power to determine the com-

pensation due, under certain circumstances, by landholders to indigo planters, and protesting that it would
be a stigma upon our judicial system ;[1] again, we meet
with an indignant note upon an unjust civil decree
passed by a native functionary : and with an elaborate
memorandum on the rights of under-tenants, for the
support of which he furnishes directions to his
assistants. These all display the practised hand of
the Secretary, guided by the now practical mind, and
closely observing eye, of the Magistrate and Collector.[2]

His administration of Azimgurh, contained, in fact,
the miniature features of his later Government of
the North-Western Provinces. He was singularly
fortunate in his Assistants, and he was not slow in
recognising their merits, and according to them his
confidence. It was indeed a rare combination of
circumstances which brought Robert Montgomery
and Henry Carre Tucker under the . magisterial
authority of James Thomason. The period he spent
in this charge was between four and five years ; but in
that time, he not only made and reported a Revenue
settlement, which gave satisfaction both to the Government and the people,[3] but gained more in knowledge

---

[1] Letter dated 5th December 1835.

[2] It is curious to observe, that now, as in after days, his main
attention was devoted to the duties of *Collector*, and that he dis-
burdened himself, as much as he possibly could, of all magisterial
business.

[3] This Settlement Report was printed in the *Journal of the Asiatic
Society* in 1837. The Sudder Board of Revenue, in reporting the
result to the Government, stated "their sense of obligation to Mr.
Thomason, who had heartily entered into their views, perfectly com-

of the country, and in the art of governing, than is commonly attained during a lifetime. To his residence at Azimgurh, he always reverted with delight; and as he visited it in his annual tours, the memory of domestic happiness, and official usefulness, could be traced in the glistening eye, and the mingled sympathies, which lighted up his countenance, or cast a shadow across it.

The demands of the State at last broke up the domestic hearth (never again to be permanently rebuilt), and the friendly social circle, of Azimgurh. The District Officer was now ripe for higher employment; and in March 1837 he was, in the most flattering manner, selected by Sir Charles Metcalfe, then Lieut.-Governor, to officiate as Secretary to the Government of the North-Western Provinces, in the Judicial and Revenue departments.[1] Within a year, however, he was compelled, by severe domestic affliction, to proceed to Europe, from whence he returned in the

prehended their plans, and carried them into execution with great skill and judgment." The assessment, like that of all the earlier settlements, was higher than the standard later adopted; but the record of rights was very carefully attended to, as well as the interests in subordinate tenures ; and the fairness of his proceedings has been justified by the great prosperity of the district, and the increase of cultivation.

[1] In the letter offering him this appointment, Sir Charles placed three posts at his disposal—a contemplated office of Commissioner or Superintendent of Settlements ; an officiating Commissionership in the regular line ; the officiating Secretaryship.

In the previous year Sir Charles had addressed a letter complimenting him highly on his administration of Azimgurh, offering him the contemplated Judgeship of that station, and even desiring to make

beginning of 1840. He was shortly after appointed permanently to the post which he had vacated.

In this Secretariat office, he served in all about two years and a half, and added further to his experience by an intimate official connection with Sir Charles Metcalfe, Mr. Robertson, and Lord Auckland who for some time administered the Government of Agra. The busy duties of Secretary did not prevent his turning attention to subjects of general interest. He inquired carefully into the nature and effect of the transit dues in the Saugor territories, and advocated their abolition (a measure which, mainly through his endeavours, was eventually carried by the Governor-General in 1847); while his ability on educational subjects was recognised by his appointment as Visitor to superintend the Agra and the Delhi Colleges.

Towards the close of 1841 he was nominated an Extra Member of the Sudder Board of Revenue, and succeeded to the permanent post, in succession to Mr. R. Merttins Bird. · In this responsible position, his versatile mind found no lack of subjects of commanding interest; and as he journeyed about the land, examining with his own eye the records of the Settlement, which was now on the eve of completion, the present writer well remembers the intuitive glance

him at once the Judge, Magistrate, and Collector of the Zillah. Mr. Thomason, however, preferred to continue simply as Collector, that he might finish his settlement, and at the same time expressed his opinion to be now against the combination (which he would seem at some former period to have favoured) of the office of Judge with that of District Officer.

that singled out the weaker portions of the work, and the sagacity and kindness with which remedies were suggested.

While Thomason held this post at Allahabad, Lord Ellenborough formed his acquaintance, and recognised his merits. He appointed him a member of the famous Finance Committee ; and soon after (about the close of 1842) selected him for an office of equal emolument to the one he held, but of greater renown, that of Foreign Secretary to the Government of India. In this capacity he accompanied Lord Ellenborough to the North-West, and finally returned with him to Calcutta. The following year, that nobleman, with full experience of his eminent abilities, nominated him Lieut.-Governor of the North-Western Provinces ; and on the 12th December 1843, the Honourable James Thomason assumed the Government.

As Lieut.-Governor, the chief seat of Mr. Thomason's residence was Agra ; but excepting the first year of his appointment, and 1848–49 (when military operations rendered carriage scarce and valuable), he spent every winter living under canvas, and marching through some portion of his territories. He also passed at Simlah the summer seasons of four years, during which, what with his tour and sojourn in the Hills, Agra did not see much of her chief.[1]   But it was ill-health

---

[1] Those summers were 1847, 1849, 1850, and 1851. It was his intention to have spent the hot season of 1854 at Nynee Tal, the mountain retreat of Rohilkund and Kemaoon.

on one occasion, and the convenience of proximity to the Governor-General on the others, that led him to Simlah; for he rather preferred to remain at Agra, where, besides other advantages, his library and records presented greater facility of reference.

The eight annual progresses accomplished during his administration were so laid out, that most of the districts were, after regular periods, visited no less than three times. The arrangements of the coming march were usually concluded two or three months before its commencement; and so exact were the details, and adhered to with such punctuality, that the time of his arrival at any stage could be depended on by every officer with almost perfect certainty. The progress of the camp might be delayed by inclement weather for one or two days, but the loss would easily be made up by forced marches, and punctuality again restored.

One great secret of Thomason's successful administration was the improvement of the opportunities afforded by these annual tours. As he rode along, attended by his staff and some of the officers of the district, by the Commissioner of the division (if sufficiently young and agile for horse exercise), and possibly by some adventurous Junior Member of the Board of Revenue, you would see a cavalcade approach. It is the Magistrate and Assistant of the new district on which you are entering, followed by the Tehseeldar and a few other officials. After greetings exchanged, for the two parties have not met since the last

triennial progress, the officers of the last district take
their leave, and the Lieut.-Governor continues his
progress. A few miles ahead, the white battlements of
a bridge are perceived through the mango-groves; and
as the party approaches, they find themselves thread-
ing the narrow roadway of a high embankment,
pierced here and there with bridges for the drainage
of the lovely lowlands, which on either side stretch
far away into the distance. Midway is the silvery
track of the main stream winding along the centre of
the plain and spanned as you pass by many noble
arches, which render its passage, formerly a difficult
and sometimes dangerous work, now of easy accom-
plishment at all seasons of the year. The minor
works are here and there minutely inspected, and the
position and safety of the embankment discussed with
the Commissioner and the Engineer of the Division,
both of whom, as arranged on the previous tour, have
given the Magistrate counsel and aid. Arrived at the
central bridge, the party descend to the stream; and
here, at the motion of the Magistrate, the head mason
of the establishment, to whose faithfulness and in-
genuity the finish and solidity of the structure are
mainly due, steps forward. The merits of the building, the causes of occasional failure, the remedies
applied, the chances of future stability or dilapidation,
are thoroughly examined. Each of the agents in the
work, not forgetting the artizan, receives his meed of
praise, and is encouraged to future exertion by the
approving word and smile of the Chief.

The cavalcade passes on to the suburbs of a populous town; the winding streets of its closely built wards have already been surveyed and mapped by the Road Engineer, for the Grand Trunk line passes through it, and the Lieut.-Governor thinks that the safety of life and limb, in the swift and constant traffic, requires a wider space and a less crooked course than the bazaar presents. The anxious shopkeepers look on with dismay, but the interests of the few must bend to those of the many, and this sharp angle, and that narrow passage, are doomed to crumble before the necessities of the State.

A little onwards is a vacant space; and here a Native gentleman, who has lately joined the party, comes forward. On this spot he proposes to build a Caravanserai, but he requires some immunities from the Government, which the Magistrate hesitates to recommend. The quick eye of the Lieut.-Governor recognises the appropriateness of the spot and the advantages of the plan. The privileges are conceded, and the next progress witnesses a spacious and substantial building for the shelter and comfort of the crowding passengers.

The Tehseelie school, filled with eager and intelligent faces, is now visited. The kind and benignant smile removes the awe with which the Ruler is regarded; and the teacher is cheered, and the boys stimulated, in their respective tasks, by seasonable advice and hearty encouragement.

Here a newly-erected Tehseeldaree engages attention; there the police-houses on the Grand Trunk road, which, with the regularity of mile-stones (but only half as frequent), ever and anon strike the eye of the carriage inmate, while they give security and assurance to the foot-traveller. Farther on lies a refractory village, lately the scene of uproar and confusion: the records of its rights and liabilities have now been adjusted, and the prosperity shining over its cultivated fields gives assurance to the Lieut.-Governor that satisfaction has been afforded.

The way now winds around ravines, and passes up and down over the high and difficult banks of a deep-lying stream. Here is met the Superintendent of the district roads, a quondam Serjeant who points out the track he has surveyed under the Magistrate's orders. The Lieut.-Governor suspects a course of intercepted drainage, and suggests another line, along which the watershed appears to run. On the next tour the same locality is hardly to be recognised in the wide and gradual descent to the well-bridged river.

The encampment happens to be pitched within a few miles of the Ganges Canal. In the cool of the evening, the party issue forth, on elephants and on horseback, and make for a bridge where a fall and a series of locks are under preparation. The heaps of kunker rock, intended to break the descent of the waters, the position and construction of the locks, the character of the masonry, all pass under the narrow inspection of the Lieut.-Governor, who observes perhaps that the neighbouring houses crowd too closely on the allotted margin, and directs the enclosure of a larger space.

The Station, a heavily populated cantonment, is reached, of which the drainage has long been a reproach, and the bane of the fine European soldiery there cantoned. The canal now passes in the vicinity : can its agency, or the neighbouring Revenue Survey, be brought to bear upon a remedy? The Station Officers, the Executive Engineer, the Road Engineer, the Canal and the Civil Officers, all meet to discuss the question : a plan is digested, and put in train by the Lieut.-Governor himself.

The new buildings and improvements in the Native city are inspected. The Dispensary is visited, and its records examined; the Apprentices are questioned; the Surgeon is encouraged to enlarge his charitable designs, and the Sub-Assistant is stimulated to prosecute with redoubled diligence and kindness his beneficent profession.

Such is but a specimen of the advantages of local inspection and personal supervision, in imparting influence, shape, and precision to the commands of Government, and inspiring the whole subordinate agency with life, intelligence, and energy. The out-of-door labour, however, formed but a trifling fraction of the operations. All reports of the district, throughout the past year or two, involving doubtful points or principles of unusual importance, were reserved for the occasion, and are now brought forward to be disposed of, discussed, or reconsidered. Difficult cases, in

3

which the District Officer was embarrassed by perplexities, or weighty matters in which the Commissioner hesitated to act before knowing the views of
his Chief, are now submitted for the advice or the
decision of the Lieut.-Governor. Further, such points
as inquiry or conversation suggested to Mr. Thomason
himself as requiring special aid, supervision, or explanation, are brought forward, and the documents
bearing on them promptly produced. All these are
carefully studied, and the questions discussed, where
necessary, with the District Officer and his subordinates,
the Commissioner, the Judge, or, as the case might
be, with the Executive Engineer or the Civil Surgeon. The results of each important deliberation
were generally embodied in a minute, or despatch, by
which, while the constituted channels of business
were respected, authority was specially conveyed, and
provision, where necessary, forthwith made, for the
prompt execution of the determined line of conduct.

An incidental advantage, but one of peculiar value,
was the acquaintance imparted by such intimate converse, with the qualifications and abilities of every
officer subordinate to the Government. Thomason
possessed a rare power of discriminating character,
and no opportunity was so favourable for exercising
it, as to find a man in the midst of his daily work.
With unexpected rapidity, the Lieut.-Governor would
perceive the weak point of a case or line of procedure;
and the officer, if not thoroughly master of his work,
would find himself foiled by one whom he counted

upon as a stranger to his business, but who turned out
to be more thoroughly acquainted with its details than
himself.   The earnest worker, and the aspiring subordinate, were recognised and encouraged.   The *former*
would be incited to prosecute, with redoubled energy,
some occupation of his own devising, or one for which
his Chief perceived in him a peculiar aptitude and
taste : here the reins would be loosened, and a generous
spur given to the willing labourer.   To the *latter*,
some special sphere of industry or research would be
suggested—perhaps, the inquiry into an interesting
custom or tenure brought to notice in the circuit : he
would be invited probably to embody his investigation
when completed, and state his views and conclusions,
in a written form ; and the impulse thus given to
talent and application, would prove perhaps the start-
ing-point of a useful, if not distinguished, career.

At home or in the camp, in the Hills or at Agra,
the same continuous course of unwearying labour was
pursued by Thomason.   The daily influx of reports
was usually disposed of promptly upon their receipt.
Such despatches as needed consideration, were reserved
for the early hours of the succeeding day, or other
leisure time.   The rapidity with which these were
mastered—no important part of the correspondence,
however long or intricate, escaping his keen eye—and
the promptitude with which appropriate orders, often
involving detailed and extended arrangements, were
issued, could not fail to impress every functionary in

the vicinity with a profound conviction of his great administrative talent. The most diverse subjects, from a riot to a district survey, from a revenue settlement to the details of a bridge, a jail, or a road, were handled with equal facility. The embryo idea of a useful scheme, perhaps almost unconsciously expressed, would immediately be caught up, and if capable of practical development, fashioned into mature existence. Independently, too, of suggestions from without, there was a creative power within, spontaneously originating new measures and designs, with a fertility of invention that betokened a mind ever restless, and active for the good of the Government. Endowed with such powerful and versatile talents, Thomason yet sought assiduously for the opinion and advice of others wherever available. A great portion of his day was spent in official interviews with officers, civil and military, connected in any way with the advancement of his administration. Social visits and parties of ceremony were equally turned, as occasion offered, to the same great object; and he used to remark, that the busy employment of such opportunities was one of the most important parts of his duty. Though he invited discussion, sought for the views of others, and desired that his own should be subjected to the severest criticism, and although he weighed most dispassionately the arguments adduced from whatever quarter, yet it was seldom, indeed, that he found occasion to alter a conviction or a conclusion once deliberately formed. Whenever he did so, he was forward to make the due acknowledgment; for no man ever grudged less to avow himself indebted to others; and the labours of his subordinates were all the more unsparingly entered upon, because, whatever value they bore, the Lieut.-Governor was the first to perceive and to reward; such generous appreciation, accorded by one who ever exhibited a lively interest in the success and the welfare of his subordinates, elicited from them a grateful response; and he received, in consequence, that ready and devoted service —the fruit of a loving and admiring spirit—which is incomparably more valuable than the forced obedience of fear and constraint.

It is no wonder, that with such powers of discernment, with so great an aptitude for business, with such a command over the services and affections of his subordinate officers, and such complete devotion to his Government, the administration flourished under his hands. No wonder that the indolent were stimulated to exertion, the able and energetic prompted to additional effort, and the careless driven by shame, if not by apprehension, to industry and reform. Praise indeed would often carry with it a higher reward than promotion (albeit the two bore ever a close connection); while animadversion and reprimand were frequently accompanied by a moral stigma that stung more pungently than actual degradation.

We propose now to examine with some detail certain of the chief proceedings by which Mr. Thomason rendered his administration so worthy of admiration.

The REVENUE DEPARTMENT is that to which his attention was earliest turned, and from which it was never averted. About the time he assumed the Government, the Circular Orders of the Sudder Board of Revenue (for the broad principles, liberal views, and lucid instructions of which, we are mainly indebted to the lamented R. Merttins Bird) fell out of print, and the want began to be felt. Instead of issuing a new edition, it occurred to Mr. Thomason to compile a fresh set of directions which, supplying what was deficient in the Board's rules, should exhibit —the whole duty of a Revenue Officer, and the principles on which our system is founded.[1] The publication, consisting originally of three parts, commenced in 1844, and the whole was completed in 1848. Of each part there were at first printed "a few trial copies, struck off for *private* circulation, in order" (as it was his constant object) "to elicit opinions on the

---

[1] In the preface to this work, after referring to the Regulations and Acts of Government in its legislative capacity and the orders issued in its executive capacity, the rules and constructions of the Sudder Court, of the Revenue Board, the Accountant, and the Civil Auditor, the Lieut.-Governor proceeds :—

"The object of the present work is to collect together, from these different sources, all that bears on the Revenue Administration of the North-West Provinces, to arrange it methodically, and to place it authoritatively before the officers employed in the department, with such additional remarks and directions, as may suffice to explain the mutual relation and dependence of the several parts of the system."

So, after enumerating the four printed Circulars of the Sudder Board of Revenue, he adds :—

"These orders were clear and succinct, and were found to be of the greatest benefit in facilitating the transaction of public business. They were, however, in their nature, incomplete, for they did not

important subjects " discussed.[1]   They were eventually published under the title of *Directions to Settlement Officers* and the *Directions to Collectors*, as conveying, in an authoritative manner, the views and instructions of the Government.   Both were subsequently re-published together,[2] with an elaborate introduction (to which Mr. Thomason appended his own name), descriptive of the "Land Revenue Administration prevalent in the North-Western Provinces of Hindustan."   It is there held, that though symptoms of proprietary right may exist under Native governments, yet they are seldom recognised, and are really superseded by the right of the State, which, taking all that it can and leaving no certain profit, deprives the private title of any recognisable, or at any rate of any marketable, value.   Our system, by limiting the demand of the Government, has virtually *created* a property in the soil.   Various phases of right are found to exist, or have grown up under us.   The

treat systematically the subjects to which they had reference, but were only a digest, under convenient heads, of orders which had from time to time been issued to meet exigencies as they arose.   In process of time, also, some of the rules were abrogated or modified.   When, therefore, a new edition of these Circular Orders was required, it was evident that extensive additions and modifications would be necessary to adapt them to the existing state of things, and it was ultimately determined to reconstruct the whole in the present form, embodying in the work such of the orders as remained in force, or throwing them into the appendices."—*Directions to Revenue Officers*, Preface, p. 4.

[1] " Preliminary Notice" to one of the Trial Copies.

[2] Under the title, *Directions to Revenue Officers*, etc., in 1850.   See title prefixed to this Article.   Several editions of an Urdu translation of both parts separately, and of the whole treatise together, have also issued from the press.

Government itself; the whole body of the cultivators; a portion of that body; the head man of the village; or a middleman; may any one of them possess the exclusive right of managing the township, or some portion of that right. Hence the necessity of not simply fixing the Government demand, but of ascertaining by whom, in what capacity, and with what rights and responsibilities, the revenue so limited is to be paid. This cannot be effected by ordinarily constituted Courts, for the endless shades of right are not susceptible of any but the most general legislative provision; and each case must therefore be separately inquired into and adjusted by a commission specially endowed with an authority at once judicial and discretionary. Such is the Court of the settlement officer. In the Treatise which follows this disquisition, the rules to be observed in the formation of settlements are carefully laid down. They differ chiefly from those of the Sudder Board in a more elaborate and philosophical definition of the rights of those connected with the soil, and more detailed directions for their ascertainment and record.

The second treatise, or the *Directions to Collectors*, embraces all the variety of duty which devolves on that most important, but ill-named, class of functionaries. It opens with general instructions for the employment and considerate treatment of Subordinates; it proceeds to lay down valuable rules for the punctual realisation of the Revenue, for limiting interference by Government and thus obliging the people as much as possible to self-management; and in case of unavoidable interference, for exercising it so as least to harass, and most to benefit, those concerned.

The following extracts show with what care Mr. Thomason inculcated kindness towards the native officials :—

"Every effort should also be used to render the performance of their duties as little as possible burdensome to them. The officer, who keeps them long in attendance at his house, or who requires that they perform their ordinary duties in court in a painful standing position, cannot derive from them that degree of assistance which would otherwise be rendered. He should so dispose his own time, and make his official arrangements, as may conduce to their comfort, and make their work light. The practice of frequently imposing fines for trivial offences cannot be too strongly deprecated. It affords an excuse for dishonesty, and for that cause often fails to have any effect. Errors of judgment should never be so punished, and corrupt or dishonest actions deserve a very different punishment, and cannot be thus either appropriately or beneficially noticed. In cases of neglect or disobedience of orders, the imposition of a fine may be salutary, but it should be moderate in amount—the offence should be undoubted, and generally the first transgression of the kind can more appropriately be noticed by recorded reproof and warning."

And again—

"Great care should be taken to maintain the respectability of the Tehseeldars. They should be selected with discrimination, and after inquiry into the goodness of their character, as well as their official capacity. They should always be received and treated with consideration, and confidentially consulted, as far as conveniently practicable, on all subjects connected with the districts entrusted to their charge. Reproof or censure, when necessary, should be given privately rather than publicly ; and, so long as they are allowed to retain office, they should be treated with the confidence and respect which is due to their high station. The occasions are very rare, in which the imposition of a fine upon a Tehseeldar is advisable or even justifiable."—*Directions to Collectors*, pp. 187–189.

Of the remaining portion of this invaluable treatise,

we shall refer only to the third section, which enforces the system for registration of landed property. A former paper in this *Review* [1] has explained, in considerable detail, the minute record both of proprietary and tenant right, which it was one great object of the revenue settlement to form. The first design of the section is to show in what manner this record can be amended and perpetuated, so as to be constantly correspondent with the daily mutation of possession and of right. The anatomy of the Collector's record-room, and the practical directions for every step, from the papers of the Village Accountant, to the archives of the Collector's office, betray the eye and the hand itself familiar with every operation described. But the most important instructions are those which exhibit how the too frequent defect of record at settlement can now be remedied. For those who possess any acquaintance with the subject, the following paragraphs will show the style and spirit, with which able officers were invited to enter upon an arduous undertaking :—

"245. It would be vain to suppose that all which is necessary has already been done. The original record, formed at the time of settlement, was often erroneous and imperfect, and it could not be otherwise. At the time of settlement the system was new and imperfectly organised ; the persons selected for its performance were not always the best qualified ; and the work was necessarily performed with far more rapidity than was compatible with accuracy. The mass of the people were ignorant, and unable to comprehend the object or nature of the proceedings, or the bearing on their position

---

[1] See Article IV. in No. XXIV. of the *Calcutta Review*, on the Settlement of the North-Western Provinces.

of the settlement, and they were moreover suspicious of any measures connected with the assessment of their lands. Under these circumstances, it is surprising that so much was done, and well done, at the time of settlement. There is far more reason to take courage from the great progress already made, than to despair at the magnitude of what still remains to be done.

"246. Let us suppose an intelligent officer appointed to the charge of a district, where he is likely to remain for some years. He is acquainted with the system of registration, and convinced of the importance and practicability of maintaining it. On coming, however, to refer to his settlement records in cases that casually occur, he finds them imperfect or erroneous. He concludes that registers resting on such a basis must be defective, and he determines to apply himself in earnest to the correction of the errors. It is the design of the present treatise to aid him in such an undertaking, and to show that it is not difficult at any time to make a fresh commencement, and to attain that degree of accuracy, which it was designed to ensure at the time of settlement.

"247. He will find the necessary powers conferred upon him by resolution of the Government, dated September 12, 1848, which is given in the Appendix, No. XXV. In this resolution are defined the limits within which the powers are to be exercised, and the precautions to be observed in the conduct of the investigations. In order to obtain the full support of his superiors in the Revenue Department, it will be necessary for him to show that he is aware of the nature and extent of the work that is before him, and of the method in which it should be performed.

"248. His first efforts should be directed to the instruction of his Sudder Omlah, and of both the pergunnah and village officers, in the system of record and registration prescribed by the Government. Great facilities have been lately afforded for the instruction of all classes of people in the peculiarities of the system, by publishing treatises on the subject in the vernacular languages, and by the series of elementary school-books in Urdu and Hindi which are designed to lead the pupils to this very subject, viz., the comprehension of the putwarris' papers. The revenue system, when rightly understood and properly worked, affords the greatest stimulus to the general education of the people. Indeed it cannot be expected that the registration of rights will ever become perfect, till the people are sufficiently educated to understand it, and to watch over its execution. There is reason, however, to apprehend, that with all the means of information that are now available, a considerable time will elapse before it can be taken for granted that even the higher and better paid class of officers, such as Serishtadars, Tehseeldars, and Canoongoes, are sufficiently familiar with the system, to enable them to judge whether the record of a mouzah has been accurately formed, or to cause its correction where it may be faulty.

"249. When the Collector is satisfied that the agents, whom he is to employ, possess the requisite degree of knowledge, he will endeavour to ascertain through their means how far the existing records are defective. Lists should be prepared of those mouzahs, in which it is most necessary to amend, or wholly to recast the record. Some will probably be found, in which remeasurement of the lands, and the formation of an entirely new misl is urgently required.

"250. Several opportunities will occur, when remeasurement and recasting of the whole records is necessary, and can be enforced, such as the division of an estate, or its being held kham for a balance. These opportunities should be seized, and the remedy applied. There are other cases where disputes of the people, or partial injury to the estate, will render the people willing to remeasure the estate, and recast the papers at their own cost. These are likely to be the cases in which such a process is the most necessary. Every effort should be used to carry it on, so as to be least expensive to the people, and so as to expose them to the least annoyance. Pains should also be taken to explain to the people the benefit they will derive from the measure, and the uses to which it may be put. The field work should be prosecuted as much as possible in the cold weather, when the Collector can give it his personal superintendence. If he cannot himself be near to control and supervise, a properly qualified subordinate officer should have the duty entrusted to him.

"251. It is most probable that he will thus, in the course of a short time, by address and management, be able to correct all the records which most need correction, without any expense whatever to the State. Each such new record will afford, as it were, a fresh start to the entries in the malgoozaree and pergunnah register regarding the mouzahs, and to the whole of the putwarris' papers. The operation will in fact consist in the formation of a new set of putwarris' papers, based on the judicially ascertained state of property in the village at the time, and not deduced from the record of a former year, as is ordinarily the case. The opportunity will not have been lost of instructing the putwarris in the discharge of their duties, and of pointing out to the people how much their welfare depends on themselves understanding the putwarris' accounts, and being careful to ensure their accuracy. If the people do not seem willing at first to remeasure their estates and correct their records at their own expense, it may be necessary to apply to superior authority for

permission to aid the work on the part of the Government, by
charging, in the contingent bill, a part or the whole of the expense
in some mouzahs, where the people are the poorest, or the most
averse to the proceeding. It has been found in some districts that
the putwarris may be instructed with little difficulty to measure the
land, prepare field maps, and perform all the work of experienced
ameens."

The resolution of Government, referred to in the
247th paragraph, confers upon all Collectors and Deputy
Collectors in these provinces, the power of "completing the record of rights in land, which should have
been made at the time of settlement, and to correct
the existing record, whenever it is found at variance
with fact." This involves the exercise, under Regulations VII. of 1822, and IX. of 1833, of a large
discretion; and where exercised with the care and
caution here inculcated by the Lieut.-Governor, there is
no reason to believe that results other than the most
beneficial have followed. Yet the indiscriminate
appointment to the duty of all Collectors and Deputy
Collectors, irrespective of their fitness and capacity for
it, has led, it may be feared, to the too summary, and
sometimes careless exercise of powers, which involve
deeply important questions of property and possession.

During the last year of his administration, Mr.
Thomason put every effort in force to introduce into
his jurisdiction the system so admirably devised and
matured in the Punjab, by which village Putwarris
are enabled, with rude implements, and yet with a
degree of scientific accuracy, to survey their boundaries,
and protract their fields upon scale. He at once perceived the vast advantages of the scheme in providing

a simple and uncostly machinery, by which the records might not only be cured of the defects of the original survey and settlement, but made effectually to keep pace with the busy changes of time. He regarded this as an important step also in native education, and endeavoured to connect it with the system of village schools under Mr. H. S. Reid's care. We have here a fine instance at the close of his career, of readiness to recognise means contrived by others, and of superiority to prejudice in casting aside the older system which had grown up under his own hands, and heartily and thankfully adopting the new.

There is but one other point in his Revenue Administration, to which we shall specifically refer : it is the position of *Talukdars*, that is, of persons claiming one or more villages, or a large tract of villages, in virtue of a superior right by conquest, by submission of the people, or by imperial grant. The claim is frequently contested by the village residents under the title of Zemindars, Biswahdars, or Mocuddums. The utmost variety of opinion has divided the Revenue authorities as to which of these parties is best entitled to be acknowledged proprietor. It was at last ruled, with the concurrence of the Sudder Court, that it is possible for two species of proprietary right, differing essentially in kind, to co-exist in the same village,—that of Talukdar as *superior*, that of Biswahdar or Mocuddum as *inferior*. The law leaves it in the discretion of the executive power to decide with which, among any number of proprietors, the

Settlement (involving the management of the estate) shall be made. Those who leant to the Talukdar, recognised *him* as either sole Zemindar, or as the manager with the Biswahdars holding dependently of him:—those again who leant to the Biswahdars, either installed them in exclusive proprietary right, or acknowledging the title of the superior, set him aside with a money allowance, and concluded all the fiscal arrangements direct with the inferior proprietors. Thomason belonged to the latter class; and as his earnest spirit never suffered him to indulge in half measures, but led him to follow out his principles to their extreme limit of appliance, it was held by some (who sided with neither of the extreme parties), that in anxiety to do justice to the claims of the Biswahdars, he was backward to acknowledge the just rights, or fulfil the reasonable expectations, of the Talukdars. This bias may be perceived in his decision, embodied in an elaborate minute recorded early in his government, by which the standard of remuneration to excluded Talukdars was to be reduced, after the death of incumbents, from $22\frac{1}{2}$ per cent. to 10 per cent. upon the Government Juma.[1] Similar principles guided

---

[1] The minute is dated the 17th January 1844. The question was long before the Court of Directors, whose decision Thomason awaited, though with full persuasion of the justice of the act, yet with some doubt as to the result. The Court eventually disallowed the reduction during the currency of the settlement, wherever it was not borne out by express stipulation, but decreed that it should thereafter take effect.

It is remarkable that this order arrived only a few weeks after Mr. Thomason's demise.

him in the settlement of resumed rent-free lands, in which the claims of the resident community, wherever supported by any vestige of proprietary possession, were preferred to the exclusion of the Maafidars. But in this instance, we have little sympathy with the excluded party, for the former Government in conferring the Maafi tenure of lands already occupied, could evidently dispose of its own right alone to the imperial share of the produce, and not of any further interests which remained, or ought to have remained, unaffected by the grant.

Time would fail, if we were to refer in any detail to the excellences of Thomason's Revenue Administration—to some of the most striking despatches, for instance, in which he provided for an equable and moderate assessment; for an efficient distribution of establishments; for the convenient adjustment of intermingled boundaries and jurisdiction; for the due enforcement of the Customs revenue (which under him reached an unwonted prosperity); for the preparation of district maps, English and Vernacular, showing all the village boundaries; for perfecting the system of proprietory records, and rendering them accessible to the public; for the survey and disposal of waste lands; for the settlement of disputed rights; for encouraging industry and the investment of capital by the conferment of a good title where none existed; for the improvement and elevation, in fine, of each branch of that complicated machinery, through which the Indian Collector touches the people. It will readily be imagined from what has been said, that his administration was vigorous and singularly successful ; that while it descended to the minutest detail, it equally grasped the most comprehensive results ; and that not only its current concerns were conducted on a liberal and sagacious policy, but that the provident eye of the Lieut.-Governor, seeing in advance of the present, laid down a mass of enlightened principles ; —principles which, if duly observed, cannot fail to guide in the future, and to extend the blessings of his administration far beyond its immediate influence.[1]

The Department of PUBLIC WORKS is the next we shall refer to, as peculiarly prominent under Thomason's Government. Endowed with a taste for mathematics, and with an engineering eye, he assumed a more decided authoritative part in all public works undertaken or proposed, than an unprofessional person

[1] For some years he had been engaged upon a "Revenue Code," embracing the principles and procedure enunciated in the *Directions*, and followed in our present system of revenue administration. He had advanced a considerable way upon this work, when he was obliged by other occupations to abandon it. It is replete with sound principles, and the dictates of much experience and judgment.

Mr. Thomason's fame, as a Revenue Administrator, was recognised and done homage to, without the bounds of his own Government. He was consulted by the Administrators of other territories, whose condition widely differed from the North-Western Provinces ; and from whatever quarter, whether from Arracan, from Madras, or from the Punjab, inquiries came, they received the same prompt attention and ingenious solution. Some detailed and careful reasoning, founded upon a reference of this description from Salem, a district in Madras, shows that if he had been spared he would have gone to that Presidency, ready and able to cope with the difficult revenue questions which perplex the Government.

4

would in general be warranted to take. Towards the remodelling of the Department of Public Works, which, instead of the dilatory and feeble machinery of a Board, should give him the prompt counsel and energetic supervision of an able Chief Engineer in immediate connection at once with himself and with all the works in progress, he wistfully looked as a great onward step, both for the improvement of the country and for relieving the Administration of a professional responsibility hardly attaching to its position. He was not spared to see that change; for even yet it only looms in the distance, though we trust its realisation draws speedily near.[1] Deprived of a professional and responsible counsellor, Thomason did not shrink from assuming the exercise of immediate and independent action wherever necessary. His admirable skill was manifest in the most intuitive perception of the

---

[1] In a despatch to the Government of India, dated the 7th June 1847, urging the appointment of a Chief Engineer, with reference to Lord Hardinge's sanction of an unlimited expenditure for the Ganges Canal, Mr. Thomason thus describes his position as Lieut.-Governor :—

"The necessary effect of the present state of things, is that in the superintendence of many public works, the Lieut.-Governor is thrown entirely on his own resources. Works involving much engineering skill are at present under construction in Rohilkhund, in Agra, in Nimar, as well as all over the country, under the Magistrates and Local Committees ; and in forming an opinion upon these, the Lieut.-Governor is forced to depend upon his own knowledge, or the casual assistance which personal friends ungrudgingly afford. But he has no fixed responsible adviser, to whom he could at all times authoritatively refer, and on whose judgment he could implicitly rely."

No doubt the strong, but just, statement of the case contained in this address, was effectual in bringing the subject to the favourable notice it is now receiving from a liberal administration.

practicability and usefulness, or otherwise, of any project laid before him. After a deliberate survey of the plans and proposals, he promptly admitted or rejected the scheme. If acknowledged to be useful, and yet perhaps immature and uncertain in its details, directions would be given for further inquiry and development ; the papers, if sufficiently important, would be published, and discussion invited ;[1] or the whole project would be thrown into the hands of some one of undoubted capacity, either to work into shape or to carry into effect. To every officer connected with the civil administration of the North-West Provinces, numerous instances will occur of important works brought to a successful issue by such happy management. He particularly watched over the proceedings of the Road and Ferry Fund Committees, and liberally fostered every useful scheme they devised. His own fertile and ceaselessly-working mind not unfrequently itself originated conceptions, which were either at once carried out, or commended to the attention and inquiries of the local officers. Thus during the past year, he projected two roads, one joining Pilibheet with Agra by a line running

---

[1] By way of illustration we may refer to a *Report on the High Road between Mhow and Saugor*, lately issued from the Agra Press, with correspondence regarding a raised, but not metalled, track proposed by Capt. Lake. The Lieut.-Governor's remarks, embodied in the concluding letter from the Agra Government, dated the 25th August 1853, will furnish a specimen of the usual and everyday orders elicited by proposals of this description. The support of the proposed line by tolls, and the necessity of obtaining the co-operation of native states, are prominently noticed.

through Bareilly and Budaon, the other uniting the Saugor territories with the Doab, *viâ* Kallinjer in the Banda district;—so as to open up to fertile but ill-accessible tracts, a new and large drain for their commodities.[1] To the Bombay and Agra road, though cramped by limited resources, he devoted a minute attention ; and one of his latest acts was to secure the approval of the Supreme Government to a scheme, by which, at increased expense, it will be rendered greatly more effective. His proposals also regarding the Mirzapore Deccan road, were carefully matured, and if carried out, would place it (though at a great expenditure) almost upon the footing of the Grand Trunk line. He took much interest in the opening of a good approach over the Sewalick range to Dera and Mussoorie, and both by public aid and private suggestion, sought to forward the undertaking. These are mentioned but as specimens : to enumerate all the important works which he originated or materially aided, would swell this article beyond all reasonable bounds.

The *Grand Trunk Road*, however, demands some

[1] The second instance here mentioned, presents a characteristic example of the mode in which Mr. Thomason treasured up, for years, the embryo of a likely scheme, till the time had arrived for its execution. The idea of the Jubbulpore road through Banda was started by Lieut. Briggs of the Engineer Corps, and communicated to Mr. Thomason in a private note, written in 1848. The public finances, or other considerations, prevented the immediate adoption of the project ; but the letter was carefully treasured, and now that obstacles to its completion were removed, was printed and circulated to all the authorities concerned, with a despatch inviting suggestions for the promotion of the design.

special remarks. Its excellent condition is mainly owing to the arrangements for constant supervision enforced by the late Lieut.-Governor. Under his sanction, small bungalows have been erected at short distances for the shelter of the Overseers; without which, frequent visits and effectual control over the native workmen, during the severity of the hot and rainy seasons, would have been impossible. His liberal policy provided a wide margin to the line, both for its own works, and the protection of the landholders from encroachment. Serious difficulty occurs in procuring *Kunkur* or metal, from lands owned by private individuals; and here the operations of the Engineers were facilitated by his wise and consistent counsels. In widening the roads and bridges, in straightening and enlarging the passage through crowded towns and bazaars, as well as in various minor arrangements for the accommodation of the trains of waggons and carriages which move upon it, he had of late instituted many marked improvements.

But the chief advance consists in the admirable protective measures, which enable the thousands of travellers to pass in security along this road, under the guardianship of a regular patrol, stationed every two miles at police posts.[1] Encamping grounds for the accommodation of troops marching on the line

[1] One of his late acts was to organise from the Ferry Funds (which he regarded as legitimately applicable to the guarding of the main roads), a large augmentation of the chowkidari force upon the Grand Trunk line. The despatch containing this order, with detailed instructions regarding the chowkidars, was printed and circulated.

have also been set aside and marked off at convenient
distances; and storehouses of wood and provisions
erected on the spot.[1] Thus not only the troops themselves march with greater comfort, but the advent of
a Regiment is not now (what we can recollect it within
the last ten or twelve years to have been) a signal to
the Tehseeldari myrmidons for extortion and oppression, enabling them to levy subsidies of grain, and to
fell the cherished trees of the people, under pretence
of supplying the troops with firewood and provisions.
Robert Montgomery has much of the credit of
maturing the scheme, and Lieut.-Colonel Steel, C.B.
(one of the most willing of Thomason's working staff),
has ably carried it out; but both needed the guiding
hand of their master.[2] Where the system is worked
with any degree of attention, it is hardly possible that
oppression of the kind alluded to can again occur.

To *Works of Irrigation*, where engineering skill is
employed directly to enhance the productive value of

[1] The encamping grounds, it has been Thomason's especial care to
have set apart in every line by which troops are accustomed to march,
and their advantages are patent as a simple expedient at once for
convenience, and for preventing encroachment on private lands and
fields. The storehouses, however, can only be put in full operation,
where the demand is sufficient to encourage speculators to contract for
the requisite supplies.

[2] Although the rules of the Supreme Government have all along
been most stringent for the full payment of all carriage, provisions,
wood, etc., required by troops, it was notorious that they were in great
measure unheeded ; and, indeed, so long as good arrangements on the
part of the Civil Officers are not in force, one can hardly blame the
half-famished sepoy, jaded by a long and weary march, for carrying
off summarily the means of satisfying his hunger. We have seen the

the soil, the comfort of the people, and their security from the ravages of famine, Thomason devoted, as it behoved an Indian Governor, an unusual share of his attention. Among his miscellaneous projects, we may allude to the survey of the environs of Delhi, organised with the object of reviving the ancient embankments of which traces still remain, as well as of procuring a record of archæological interest, — regarding the venerable capital of India. His efforts for draining the adjacent extensive swamp of Nujjufgurh, were, in the face of great difficulties, unremitting ; and though not yet entirely successful, have still received reward in the rich crops now covering the soil which has been laid bare by the escape of a portion of the waters. The operations in Ajmere have been explained to the public, both of England and of India, in Colonel Dixon's *Sketch of Mairwara*,[1] a work which owes its origin to the same suggestive mind that aided and forwarded the admirable measures there recorded. In an opposite direction, among the forests of the Rohilkhund Terai,

stores of wood, the scene of a regular storm, carried away without the thought of payment, to the sad dismay of the unfortunate supplier. The natural consequence was, that the loss fell eventually on the surrounding villages. Such practices are now unknown.

To make the wise rules of the Government of India universally known, both for the warning of the military and encouragement of the Civil officials, Thomason compiled with great care all the orders and rules bearing on the subject, and published them under the title, *Selected orders, Civil and Military, regarding March of Troops, the Mode of supplying them with Carriage, Provisions, etc., published by order of the Honourable Lieut.-Governor, N.-W. P., Agra,* 1849.

[1] See a review of this work in *Calcutta Review,* No. XXX., Art. IX.

and within sight of the snowy Himalayas, the energetic proceedings of Captain Jones for draining the
marshy lands of that exuberant but neglected tract,
and turning its precious but hitherto wasted streams
to the purposes of irrigation, were watched and
directed with equal care.[1]

The Nugeena Canal in Bijnore, and the canals of
the Dera Doon, no less than their greater and more
important rivals, the Eastern and Western Jumna
Canals, engaged his lively interest. He was ever on
the watch for suggestions to improve their efficiency ;[2]
and it is but within a few months, that his advocacy
secured the approval of the Governor-General and the
Court of Directors to a scheme upon a grand scale for
straightening, at the expense of above a lakh and a

[1] See *Calcutta Review*, No. IX., Art. III.
[2] A running memorandum of the progress of each work in repaying
its outlay, was regularly kept up among his private memoranda.
During the past year, Mr. Thomason officially called the attention
of Colonel Cautley to some valuable suggestions made privately by
him more than five years before. We quote from this despatch, as it
is another striking instance of the care with which schemes once
started were treasured up, and reserved for the proper opportunity :—
"The project of a new canal from the Song River is a promising
one. But there is another project of drawing water from the Buldi
River, above the Sansadarra, which once engaged attention, but has
apparently now been lost sight of. The notice of this project is
contained in a private note from yourself, dated March 9th, 1848. It
has been carefully kept for many years, and is now placed on record
to preserve it from oblivion." Colonel Cautley is then requested to
have both worked out, and estimates framed, so that the report might
be printed, "and remain for execution, when money and agency are
forthcoming." His attention is also called to further suggestions
made in a pamphlet published also under Thomason's authority—*Notes
and Memoranda on the Water Courses in the Dera Doon, by Captain
Cautley*, 1845.

half of rupees, the tortuous course of a portion of the Eastern Jumna Canal, thus greatly adding to its efficiency, and diminishing the cost of its maintenance.[1]

Regarding these subjects, and indeed upon all engineering questions, Thomason placed a well-deserved and unlimited confidence in Lieut.-Colonel Cautley, the Superintendent of Canals in the North-West Provinces and Director of that great work, the GANGES CANAL, which is the creation of his own genius. If interested in the comparatively puny aqueducts above alluded to, it may well be imagined that this truly imperial undertaking called forth the full tide of the late Lieut.-Governor's solicitude. Deeply persuaded of its vast importance, both in adding to the resources of the kingdom, and ameliorating throughout an immense extent of country, the horror of those famines to which the North-West Provinces, from their uncertain climate, must be constantly liable, he acted upon the principle that all lesser interests may well bend before this object of paramount necessity. It was not that he aided either in devising or in perfecting any of the engineering details; the merit of originating the

[1] As a first step towards carrying through this great work, the Superintendent was invited to mature the design and to prepare a report upon it, in a popular form, comprehensible by unprofessional readers. Permanency and publicity were given to the result of this suggestion, under the following title—*Notes on the Levels of the Eastern Jumna Canal, explanatory of a Project for completing the Regulation of the Slope of the Canal bed. 1st May 1852, Agra. By Lieut. W. E. Morton, Superintendent of the Eastern Jumna Canals.*

grand conception, and of developing its various parts, belongs to Colonel Cautley, and to him alone. But to Thomason does belong the credit, which of itself would have rendered his administration famous, of grasping the idea in all its largeness and importance, and of representing the object, and advocating the claims of the work in so powerful a manner (at the time when a stinted expenditure would have starved into insignificance the noble design, and a mistaken policy have reduced it to a mere boat canal), that the Government were persuaded to remove the restrictions imposed by Lord Ellenborough, the merits of the undertaking were fully recognised, and Colonel Cautley allowed a discretionary command of means without bound or restriction.

The GANGES CANAL is so closely connected with the administration now under review, and its approaching opening invests it with so much present attraction, that our readers will probably not be unwilling to possess a short abstract of its history.

On the 23rd of May 1838, Colonel Cautley submitted to the Government of the North-West Provinces, a series of levels taken by him a year or two before, with a view to test the possibility of pouring, for purposes of irrigation, a flood of water from the Ganges below Hurdwar into the Kali Nuddi at Bolundshuhur. Though this was reported to be impracticable, yet the idea of the Ganges Canal had dawned upon his mind, and he solicited authority to carry on his investigations for supplying water to the

" Mozuffernugger, Sirdana, and Meerut districts."[1]
The reply, written by Thomason, under Lord Auckland's authority, states that " His Lordship is not prepared to expect much success in any attempt to draw a canal from the right bank of the Ganges. If, however, the object could be attained, the public benefit would be very great. It appears from Captain Cautley's letter that the question can easily be set at rest, and it is highly desirable that it should be so without delay." The Military Board were accordingly instructed to give Captain Cautley a small establishment to prosecute his inquiries.

In 1840, Thomason, again at the Secretariat post, expressed to Captain Cautley, the Honourable Mr. Robertson's gratification at the result of his investigations, which were printed for general information. In 1841, Mr. Robertson recorded an enlightened and elaborate minute respecting the importance of the projected canal, " the practicability of which had,

[1] A little sketch accompanies and illustrates this report, and in it a pencil dotted line, marked in Colonel Cautley's writing, the "*probable direction of head*," to pass by Roorkee, exhibits the singular sagacity of that distinguished Engineer, in *seeing* as it were, where other men conjecture and calculate.

It is curious to observe, that in the reply of Government another object for which the establishment was also granted, is regarded as a much more likely and promising scheme, viz., a proposal to draw off *Rajbuhas* (or minor water-courses) from the chief rivers in the Upper Doab. These inquiries seem to have originated in a scheme of Captain Debude for irrigating from the Hindun and Kali Nuddi, but it was Colonel John Colvin, C.B., the Superintendent of Canals preceding Colonel Cautley, who left the idea of a canal from the Ganges as a legacy to his successor.—Preface to Col. Cautley's *Report on the Central Doab Canal*, 12th May 1840.

through Captain Cautley's unwearied zeal and talent, been satisfactorily established," and submitted to Lord Auckland repeated addresses, pressing the undertaking upon the Government. In the preparation of these, Thomason doubtless assisted.

On the 1st September 1841, the Court of Directors, upon a review of the whole question, and guided by the recommendation of the Indian Government, accorded their liberal sanction to the project, estimated at above a million sterling; and Captain Cautley with vigour commenced the work. But a change soon came over the spirit of the Government; for upon the 29th April 1842, Lord Ellenborough, from the military bureau, directed the suspension of existing arrangements, on account of financial and *other* considerations; and, if this were capable of misconstruction, two months later (21st June 1842), he issued positive orders from the Civil department, that pending "a further test to the scientific and financial calculations on which the scheme was based, all further expenditure was to be discontinued." It was represented, however, by the Agra Government, that to close at once all the progressing operations, would be to involve the State in a serious loss; and the Governor-General therefore consented (September 1842) that existing works might be carried on, but at the paltry expenditure of two lakhs in the year.

Things continued on this unsatisfactory footing till the beginning of 1844, Captain Cautley being obliged, from the want of subordinate agency, to conduct with his own hands the drudgery of surveying levels and such like work. It was one of Thomason's earliest acts as Lieut.-Governor to remonstrate strongly (February 1844) against this most uneconomical and extravagant misuse of the Director's time and talents—a waste of directing energy, which no private Company, acting simply for their own benefit, would have incurred. The scanty aid conceded by Lord Ellenborough in reply, was given grudgingly, and accompanied by the following strange misconception :—"*It is*," His Lordship said, "*with the view of making a canal of Navigation, that the project has been sanctioned, and that sums for constructing it have been granted. Irrigation is to be a secondary object, towards which, after the first object has been effected, the surplus waters are to be applied. His Lordship desires that this may be continually held in view.*" It is well that this Nobleman had already neutralised these false views by the appointment, as his Lieutenant, of an officer who would not shrink from exposing their fallacy ; else the Ganges Canal, for the chief end of its existence, might have sunk into utter inefficiency.

But Thomason perceived the critical position, and addressed himself with determination to do battle for the Canal. He visited the works, and after becoming thoroughly acquainted with their state, and the folly of prosecuting them in the present sluggish fashion, he promptly addressed the Governor-

General (April 1844), and boldly pleaded the issue whether His Lordship's limit could be justified upon any grounds, either of sound policy, of economy, or of humanity. Hitherto this limit had not done much injury, for in the beginning of a great design, it is long before a sufficient supply of artisans and labourers can be procured. Now, however, "the fame of the work had spread": carpenters, masons, artificers, labourers, had congregated from the most distant quarters—Oudh, Bhuttee, Marwara, etc. If the restriction be maintained, these must go away, "and the conductors of the work be discredited." Viewed in a *political* aspect, "the national reputation was pledged to its success." The many thousands assembled at the Hurdwar fair had seen the State "embarked in the gigantic undertaking" of turning the Ganges into the Doab; and if the Government were baffled in the work, the prestige of our power and credit would be shaken.[1] Again, the Government was bound by motives of *humanity* not to delay a work certified as an effectual means of saving a great tract of land from famine; yet the present sluggish rate would not complete this work within thirty or forty years to come, during the whole of which period

[1] This was a view which had evidently taken much hold of his mind ; for at the close of the following year, in reply to inquiries from the Court of Directors, he writes :—

"In the face of the whole Hindu population, assembled at the great Koomb" (or duodecennial) "fair, the British nation stood pledged to this great work, gigantic in itself, but invested with peculiar importance in the eyes of our subjects from its connection with their sacred river, and favourite place of pilgrimage."

the country would be abandoned to the inroads of drought and all its unmitigated horrors.[1] Mere *economy* demanded loudly that the operations should be expedited, in order that the expense of costly supervision might be saved. The petty two lakhs expended on it were no more than the annual net income received direct from the Jumna Canals. "Hitherto the Government have advanced nothing towards the Ganges Canal from the general resources of the State. Notwithstanding the proof daily before their eyes of the benefits arising from canals, they have just done sufficient to commit themselves to the undertaking, but have shrunk from embarking in it with that zeal and determination which will bring its benefits within their reach." The Governor-General, who could lavish his thousands upon the Somnath gates, and "the favourite sweetmeat" of the Sepoys, was moved by this potent reasoning to grant the petty — subsidy of *a single lakh more for one year !*

But the masterly State paper, of which we have given a sketch, was to receive a worthier treatment

[1] Shortly after this despatch, Mr. Thomason addressed the Military Board on another aspect of this question. Sound policy demanded that the works should be substantial and secure, and the superintendence most effective ; for after a canal had once come into full play, and had caused in its vicinity a vast increase of population, corresponding with the increased productiveness of the soil, the failure of water arising from any oversight or blunder of the Engineers, must involve the unsuspecting people in all the horrors of an *artificial* famine. (21st May 1844.) This is a most serious aspect of the case, and proves the urgent necessity of the works being efficiently officered, both as respects the *number* and *qualifications* of the supervisors.

from more discriminating hands. In 1845, it is true, Lord Hardinge postponed the more vigorous prosecution of the work, but he did so simply from sanatory considerations, in expectation of the report of a committee appointed to investigate the effect of canal irrigation upon the healthiness of the adjacent country. The Sutlej campaign called away Major Baker (who occupied the place of Major Cautley while in England) both from this committee and the canal. But the glorious success of our arms had no sooner freed Lord Hardinge from the cares of the field, than he nobly compensated for all the inaction, illiberality, and error that had preceded.

In March 1847, Lord Hardinge visited the stupendous works of the Solani aqueduct, and having thoroughly entered into all the Lieut.-Governor's sentiments, shortly after recorded a minute which reflects honour on His Lordship's name. He abandoned Navigation except as a subsidiary object, enunciated the principle that IRRIGATION was the grand design, before which every thing must bend, and declared himself ready to authorise the twenty lakhs a year, named by Major Baker,—nay to sanction "*as large a sum for future years as the Director could expend with a due regard to economy.*" [1]

The battle was now won. Minor lets and hindrances were easily overcome.[2] In 1850 the

[1] Minute by Lord Hardinge, dated 20th April 1847.

[2] About the close of 1847, both the Court of Directors and the Governor-General (Lord Hardinge), in view of the mighty proceedings in progress, expressed some hesitation; but it was readily removed

enhanced estimate of above a million and a half sterling was cheerfully passed by the Honourable Court.
And thus, under the liberal policy of the enlightened
nobleman now presiding over the Government of
India, and under the careful patronage of his Lieut.-
Governor who at every check or difficulty was ready
to advocate before his Chief the claims of the canal,
or to solve perplexities by his suggestions, the
magnificent work has progressed apace till the
present day, when, on the verge of completion, the
guiding and protecting hand, scarcely now required
more, has been suddenly removed. Thomason was
to have been present at the formal opening of the
Canal in the ensuing spring : but his work was done.
And Colonel Cautley cannot but feel that the spirit
which imparted life, energy and success to his great
design, has departed, just as the Canal in millions
of rivulets was about to pour across the vast plain
of the Doab its vivifying flood of luxuriance and
plenty.

While Thomason was only the advocate and helper
of the Ganges Canal, he was the originator of the
ENGINEERING COLLEGE AT ROORKEE.

From the first deeply he was impressed with the

by the powerful representations of the Lieut.-Governor. The revised
estimate, ungrudgingly passed by the Court of Directors, in their
despatch dated the 2nd June 1852, amounts to the enormous sum of
Rs. 1,55,48,100. Mr. Thomason used constantly to keep running
accounts of the advancing expenditure among his private memoranda.

5

necessity of providing, for the multitude of Public works throughout the country, a staff of Native engineers, possessing both professional knowledge and experience. In the beginning of 1845, he projected a scheme by which the most advanced pupils of the Agra and Delhi Colleges, or other candidates, might, under the guidance of Lieut. Baird Smith, and amid the works of the Eastern Jumna Canal, add to their theoretical attainments a sound practical acquaintance with engineering. When the details were matured, the Lieut.-Governor obtained, but not without repeated appeals, permission to extend " by way of experiment," the benefits of the proposal to three or four qualified youths.[1] Upon this was grounded the Notification of the 9th October 1845, constituting "a class of officers, to be denominated *Sub-Assistant Executive Engineers.*" The plan was found to work so well, that their number was soon increased from four to twenty.[2]

After Lord Hardinge had resolved on the vigorous prosecution of the Ganges Canal, Thomason at once perceived how this great undertaking might itself prove the nursery of such an engineering body as he longed to raise up from amongst the indigenous materials of the country. He lost no time in developing the idea, and on the 23rd September 1847

---

[1] The project was in danger of being shelved along with a proposition of the Educational Department in Bengal for the encouragement of Civil Engineering amongst the natives. But Thomason vindicated the special claims and advantages of the North-Western Provinces as a Civil Engineering School.

[2] On the 22nd December 1846.

laid his proposal before the Supreme Government.[1] He dwelt at great length on the requirements of the country ;—surveys, irrigation, application of water power, navigation, roads, bridges, railways,—objects these for all of which it was impossible to provide sufficient engineering skill. He then appealed to the Government to avail itself of the present opportunity to form a Native class :—

"The establishment now forming at Roorkee, near the Solani aqueduct on the Ganges Canal, affords peculiar facilities for instructing Civil Engineers. There are large workshops, and extensive and most important structures in course of formation. There are also a library and a modelroom. Above all a number of scientific and experienced Engineer Officers are constantly assembled on the spot, or occasionally resorting thither.

"These officers, however, all have their appropriate and engrossing duties to perform, and cannot give time for that careful and systematic instruction which is necessary for the formation of an expert Civil Engineer.

"On these accounts the Lieut.-Governor would propose the establishment at Roorkee of an Institution for the education of Civil Engineers, which should be immediately under the direction of the Local Government in the Educational Department."

In conformity with this proposal, which was

[1] Colonel Cautley had apprehended the same idea so early as 1843, when, applying for a large number of well-educated and skilful artificers, he added that "they will not only be useful in themselves, but will establish a school for the ultimate supply of efficient workmen to the whole line of the canal." What is here proposed for the Canal, Thomason organised for the whole of Hindustan.

The same letter suggests the further idea of workshops, etc., likewise followed out by Thomason. "We shall require numerous workshops, storerooms, etc., at Roorkee, which place I intend to establish the headquarters of the Ganges Canal" :—he proceeds to recount the plans of workshops, modelrooms, etc., which his busy and practical mind had already designed. — *Letter dated October* 4, 1843.

warmly supported by the Governor - General, the College was opened on the 1st of January 1848, for the instruction both of Natives and of European soldiers, and Non-commissioned Officers.

In 1851, persuaded of the success of his scheme, and fortified by the support of the Committee upon the system of Public Works,[1] and of Sir Charles Napier,[2] Thomason projected a vast enlargement of the original plan, so as to include not only greater numbers of Natives and Soldiers, but likewise Commissioned Officers, both of the Royal and Company's services; the establishment of a Depôt and Workshop for the repair of surveying and other scientific instruments;[3] a Museum of Economic Geology, an Observatory, a Printing establishment, and other appurtenances to render the Institution effective. These propositions were printed by His Honour in a brochure and submitted to the Governor - General, who accorded to them his hearty support. On the 2nd June 1852 the Court of Directors communicated their sanction,

---

[1] See their report dated 5th March 1851.

[2] "The suggestion," writes Thomason, "of admitting to the College Commissioned Officers of both services, is due to His Excellency General Sir Charles Napier, in communication with whom the present scheme has been drawn out." Its groundwork is the same as that of the Senior department of the Military College at Sandhurst, adapted to the Indian Army.—*Address to the Government of India, dated 28th August* 1850.—See also page 17 of the *Account of Roorkee.*

[3] This is a desideratum of more importance than at first sight might appear, in a country where there are no private establishments in which such instruments might be repaired. Their injury or disorder is now a continual obstacle to the advance of scientific inquiry and tuition.

and the whole scheme is now being carried into effect.

The influence which these establishments will have in the enlightenment of India and development of her resources, in the progress of civilisation and scientific inquiry, and in the advancement of the Officers and Soldiers of our army, cannot be over-estimated ; and the credit of the whole belongs to Thomason. He naturally regarded the Institution with a peculiar interest, and watched over it with a sort of parental solicitude and pride. The extensive quadrangle,[1] now being erected to complete the enlarged design, was to have been opened by him at the close of the following year, thus constituting, as it were, the last public act of his official career.

To the JUDICIAL AND CRIMINAL DEPARTMENT of his Government, the attention of Thomason was less directed than to the rest of his duties. We cannot point in it, as we can in almost every other, to any large measure of reform (excepting, perhaps, the Grand Trunk Road police), involving either present great results, or the germ of future improvement. This was partly owing to the nature of the subject, which did not involve the abstract principles with which he delighted to work, or any national institutions on which his conservative mind loved to engraft his forward movements. At one point, where those institutions were approached, they trammelled, rather

[1] See the elevation and ground-plan at page 20 of the *Account of Roorkee.*

than assisted, his views. The Chowkidar (watchman) must belong to the *Village Community* : he must be remunerated by a small holding of the village lands : he must be the servant of the Zemindar : salary paid in cash direct from Government, would loosen the Zemindar's hold upon him ; while a close surveillance of his proceedings would interfere with the independent action of the village institution. Perhaps such may be a specimen of the reasons for which he shrank from a reform of our Police system.

But it was impossible for a mind like his of whom we write, to preside over the Judicial Administration of the country, without introducing many improvements and infusing a vigour into all its movements. The distribution of his agency was, for the most part, admirable ;[1] the same prompt and searching orders were daily issued as in the Revenue Department. A careful amendment of local jurisdiction was effected

[1] In judging of this question, it must be remembered that the Covenanted agency was not of his own choosing. His task was to make the arrangement of them best suited for the good of the country. If sometimes Officers who had proved inefficient in the magisterial and revenue charge of a *District* were readily advanced to the Judicial Bench, it must be remembered that the same points which impair a Magistrate's usefulness (as want of promptitude and personal activity) do not, in an equal degree, affect a Judge, and that the hesitancy which often accompanies a high deliberative faculty, is directly prejudicial to the energetic management of a district. Nevertheless, it is possible that Thomason's leaning towards the Revenue Department may have induced him to favour it, upon. the whole, with better officers than the Judicial.

It has been asserted in some of the public prints, that Mr. Thomason had a bias to promote men of a strong religious principle. No doubt, a consistent profession of religion had its weight, among

wherever ill arrangement or intermixture impeded the administration of justice; and the subordinate agency was revised for the more efficient discharge of its duty. The Police divisions were frequently enlarged, and from the saving effected by reduction in number, the salary of the Police officers was proportionally increased. The district Dáks were fostered by him. The management of the Jails throughout the country was improved ; and the Central Prison at Agra, under Inspectors judiciously selected and guided by the Lieut.-Governor, has made an advance in prison discipline hitherto unknown in India.

A special and important feature of the administration is the extensive employment of Revenue officers in Police and Judicial posts. The Tehseeldars have, in many districts, been invested with the power of Daroga, and from their known respectability and character, have imparted a new stamp of credit and

other qualities, in his estimate of a man's character ; as profligacy or dishonesty had its share also. But as far as official requirements are concerned, we deny that a profession of religion or the reverse was an element which he took into consideration, in the distribution of patronage. High and honourable principle was the point he looked to, and wherever he found that, the only question with him for debate was the qualification of the candidates and their respective fitness for office. It is impossible that any unprejudiced man acquainted with the society of Agra, and with the chief appointments held there within the last half-dozen years, could for a moment entertain the charge. As Thomason regarded no part of his duty more onerous and unpleasant than the distribution of patronage, so we are assured that there was none which he exercised with a greater deliberation, or endeavoured to discharge with a more single eye to the welfare of the State, or a sterner conscientiousness and disregard of private friendship, feeling, and partiality.

confidence to the police proceedings. So every Deputy Collector is constituted likewise a Deputy Magistrate, and numerous Tehseeldars throughout the country have been installed in the same commanding position. The movement is undoubtedly in the right direction; but the conferment of magisterial powers has, probably, been too indiscriminate, and without a sufficient guarantee of character, or of the knowledge required for the discharge of such grave functions, affecting everywhere the social body. The point is urged with the greater confidence, because the necessity for a test of efficiency had already been conceded in the case of Covenanted Assistants, and there is no reason to stop its application there. A second objection is, that the new functions bring with them no increase of emolument, although they vastly add to the labour and responsibility, as well as to the dignity, of the officer holding them. In one district we have a Deputy Collector with the small and unimportant powers of an Assistant; in the adjoining district, his brother Deputy has special powers, involving authority of greater magnitude; in a third, he is a full Magistrate, and can not only imprison any of Her Majesty's dusky subjects for three years, but visit every Englishman who commits a trespass with a fine of 500 rupees, or in default thereof with two months' imprisonment. In one Pergunnah we have a Tehseeldar employed solely in the quiet duties of a Revenue Collector; in the next he may have any of the magisterial powers we have just enumerated.

Yet all are paid alike, without the slightest reference to their varied responsibilities. Surely this is inexpedient, if it be not unfair, and for a great Government unbecoming. The officer possessing the higher powers may be (and sometimes actually has been) remanded for neglect or misdemeanour to a *lower* grade of authority, yet no diminution of emolument ensues. Great devotion to his office may be followed by promotion to the higher grade, yet no increase of salary is gained. The Service thus loses at once the stimulus to exertion, and the salutary dread of loss and degradation; while both officers and people are taught to regard, without estimation or respect, a power and office which it ought to be our great effort to invest with dignity and with influence. Such a course cannot fail of an injurious effect upon the Government itself.

In one respect the government of Thomason has greatly benefited the Criminal and Judicial Department in common with every other, viz., by the *Publications, which under his authority were issued from the press.* Of these may be noticed the *Memoir on the Statistics of the North-Western Provinces,* by A. Shakespear, Esq., C.S., 1848 ; containing, in a condensed form, the most minute information as to the area, revenues, and population of each pergunnah and district. The results of a second Census, made also under the careful and minute instructions of the Lieutenant-Governor, on the last day of 1852, have since been published ;[1] and contain the most valuable and accurate returns yet obtained in India.

In the first year of his government, Thomason forwarded to every Magistrate and Collector an invitation to throw together all the statistical and general information he could obtain regarding his jurisdiction, to be printed in a volume illustrated by maps and statements. Such a publication, he thought, would " form an official history of each district, and contain all that would enable the public officers of Government to understand the peculiarities of the district, and conduct of the administration." Minute directions were given how to arrange the various matter,—statistical, historical, geographical, economical, educational,—regarding the current tenures, rise and fall of families, operation of special measures or laws, effect of the revenue and judicial systems, etc. Few officers have had the energy and skill to work out the plan ;[2] but the *Statistical Report of Cawnpore*, by

[1] See *Agra Gazette* of 18th October 1853. The details of this census are now in the press in a volume, by Mr. G. J. Christian, Secretary to the Sudder Board of Revenue, through the agency of which Board the work was carried out. The instructions for this Census were drawn up by Thomason himself with great pains, and no precaution was omitted for securing perfect accuracy. The whole was accomplished on the night of the 31st of December, and the result was carefully tested by the district officers and their subordinates.

[2] Only four have been yet published :—
Statistical Report of the District of Cawnpore. By R. Montgomery, Esq., C.S., 1849.
Statistical Report of the District of Goorgaon. By Alexander Fraser, Esq., C.S., 1849.
Statistical Report of the District of Futtehpore. By C. W. Kinloch, Esq., C.S., 1852.

Mr. Montgomery, illustrates the wisdom of the design, and the usefulness of such a treatise for advancing and facilitating, in every department, the administration of a district. We earnestly hope that the conception will not be lost sight of till we are furnished with a similar guide and official companion for every district in the provinces.

In other departments we may notice the *Settlement Misl* (1847), which forms a specimen of the papers required from first to last in the settlement of each of the prevailing classes of tenure, with a counterpart in English (also 1847): The *Accountant's Manual*, by C. Allen, Esq., 1847 ; The *Civil Auditor's Manual*, by T. K. Loyd, Esq., 1851 ; *Statistics of Indigenous Education*, by R. Thornton, Esq., 1850 ; and *Comparative Tables of District Establishments in the North-Western Provinces*, by A. Shakespear, Esq., C.S., 1853.[1] These were the immediate results of the instruction or suggestion of the Lieut.-Governor, and have proved,

Statistical Report of the Districts of Kemaon and Gurhwal. By J. H. Batten, Esq., C.S., 1851.
A Report for Budaon, by Mr. Court, is, we believe, now in the press, and others, more or less answering the objects in view, have been prepared for Agra and Furruckabad.

[1] This work contains a vast fund of official information. The districts and offices are classed according to their comparative difficulty and amount of business : then the salaries and cost of management in each compartment are compared for each district throughout the provinces. Wherever an office is under-officered, or underpaid, the fact cannot fail to be brought to light, and complaints of the overworked Amlah, formerly resting too much on the haphazard opinion of the recommending officer, can now be easily tested by the reasonable grounds of comparison with similar business and establishments elsewhere.

and will long continue to prove, of special use to the public service. It would too greatly extend this article to enumerate the many other issues of a less formal and elaborate nature; but there is one which we must not pass over. Thomason constantly met with valuable information and suggestions in miscellaneous reports, or scattered here and there throughout a wide correspondence; such papers had hitherto remained too often unnoticed and unknown, engulfed in the indiscriminate reservoir of all that is good, bad, and indifferent—the Secretariat Record Room. It occurred to him that, though not worthy of *separate* publication, these yet might be thrown together, and published from time to time as ——*Selections from the Records of the Government.* This work, maintained to the present day, has given a permanent and public form to a vast variety of most useful and suggestive papers on all official subjects—revenue, police, judicial, engineering, statistical; and its practical usefulness has been recognised by the adoption of the same idea, though not precisely on the same principle, by the other Indian Governments.[1]

[1] Almost all the papers that have issued under the name of "*Selections*" from the other Governments have been complete and formal reports, which, under any circumstances, would have been published by the Government of the North-Western Provinces separately, without reference to its selections, which were intended for extracts, miscellaneous papers, and scraps otherwise liable to fall into oblivion. Thomason generally indicated with his own hand the papers or extracts which he desired to publish in this series.

We must hasten to conclude this already too extended sketch by a notice of Thomason's proceedings in the EDUCATIONAL DEPARTMENT. As respected Colleges and Station Schools, the chief tendency of his proceedings was to abolish the latter and to strengthen the former. He found the funds at his disposal inadequate to provide efficiently for both, and he wisely resolved that, instead of a number of ill-officered and unsatisfactory institutions at Stations scattered over the country, the Government should have a few large and superior Colleges at convenient distances, accessible to each great division of the province. It was also his hope that, wherever Stations were thus abandoned, the field would be occupied in a more efficient manner by private effort, indigenous as well as foreign.[1]

[1] His sentiments on this subject, and their happy fulfilment with respect to one at least of the seminaries thus given up, are expressed in the following extract of an address made by the Lieutenant-Governor at the examination of the College of the American Presbyterian Mission, Allahabad, in December 1852 :—

"He said that the examination had been listened to with pleasure by all the auditors, but that to himself the display was peculiarly gratifying, because he saw before him the realisation of all those anticipations which he had previously formed regarding the Institution. A few years ago, there was a Government school maintained in Allahabad. It was well endowed by the Government; it was countenanced and encouraged by all the high officers of Government then at the place. But he judged that that, as well as other similar institutions, did not bring a benefit to the State commensurate with the charge they entailed upon it. He felt that they came into competition with other schools which would probably be maintained by private individuals without any cost to the State, and that they so far discouraged, rather than promoted, the general cause of education. He therefore abolished those schools, and concentrated the efforts of Government on the improvement of the colleges maintained in our cities, where there was ample room for many educational establish-

In the management of these Colleges, Thomason took a constant interest, and, when presiding at their public examinations, seldom failed to deliver some pertinent remarks on the bearing of our educational measures, and the manner in which his young audience should improve their opportunities. The original views and erudite labours of Dr. Ballantyne received from him a discriminating and powerful support. He acknowledged the claims which the large section of the nation devoted to the study of Sanscrit, possess upon the State to recognise and foster whatever is true and exalted in their literature; and he had a lively persuasion that when once European learning and philosophy should be presented to the Brahminical mind in a comprehensible and attractive, because indigenous dress, the influence of the learned Pundits upon the people at large would produce results of prodigious moment. He did not neglect the objections which a misapprehension of the Benares system has in some quarters created; but, on the contrary, encouraged the discussion of its merits among those best qualified to judge. Once convinced, however, of

ments. He that day witnessed the result of this measure in Allahabad. The number of pupils in the Allahabad Government School was under 100, whilst there were 327 boys on the list of the Mission School. Many of these boys had attained a high proficiency in secular learning, and they also received that which the Government abstained upon principle (and he considered justly) from imparting— sound and diligent instruction in the truths of Christianity." On this happy result he congratulated the authorities of the College, and paid a high and well-merited compliment to the successful and disinterested labours of the Mission from America.

the justness of Dr. Ballantyne's position, he yielded him, despite of narrow-minded or utilitarian opposers, an unflinching support, to which, on the opening of that magnificent structure—the BENARES COLLEGE— raised under his administration, he gave a public and unqualified expression.[1]

[1] The sentences in which Thomason alluded in the opening of the College to Dr. Ballantyne's labours are important, and deserve to be here extracted :—

"Dr. Ballantyne assumed charge of the College in the beginning of 1846, and avowed as his object the formation of a class of Pundits, who, skilled in all that is taught in native schools, should also have their minds so tinctured with European habits of feeling, as to be pre-eminent among their countrymen. In order to accomplish this object, he first himself mastered the Hindu Philosophy, and he ascertained how much of truth there was in it, and where error commenced. He, at the same time, made available to his Pundit pupils the work of European philosophers, and showed, by treatises of his own composition, how, advancing from the premises of Hindu philosophy, the correct conclusions of European philosophy might be attained. In following this course, he acted in consonance with the whole character of our administration in this country. We have not swept over the country like a torrent, destroying all that it found, and leaving nothing but what itself deposited. Our course has rather been that of a gently swelling inundation, which leaves the former surface undisturbed, and spreads over it a richer mould from which the vegetation may derive a new verdure, and the landscape possess a beauty which was unknown before.

"There is every reason why a similar course should be pursued in philosophy and literature. We have not found the people of this country an ignorant or simple race. They were possessed of a system of philosophy which we could not ignore. Some persons, in the pride of political superiority, may affect to despise it ; but it has roused the curiosity and excited the wonder of the learned in all countries of Europe. Dr. Ballantyne's publications enable the most superficial reader to discover that it possesses a depth of thought, a precision of expression, and a subtlety of argument which are amongst God's choicest gifts to His creatures. These may be misused, but they may be also reclaimed, and devoted to the highest purposes."—*Speech delivered at the opening of the Benares College on the* 11*th January* 1853.

But the measure which bears the peculiar stamp of Thomason's mind, and which, perhaps more than any other hitherto devised, will tend to the enlightenment and welfare of India, is the system established by him for encouraging the VERNACULAR AND INDIGENOUS SCHOOLS of the country.

In 1845, the Lieut.-Governor forwarded to every Magistrate and Collector in the Provinces a circular order, in which, while they were generally charged with fostering the Village schools, instructions were given to ascertain and report the extent to which such institutions imparted education to the people. These directions, grounded on the plan pursued by Mr. Adam in Bengal, were, like all others emanating from Thomason's pen, so clear and practical, that within two or three years, a complete return of the whole educational institutions in the country was obtained.[1]

In 1846, the Lieut. - Governor addressed the Supreme Government, stating as the result of these inquiries, that, " on an average, less than 5 per cent. of the youths who are of an age to attend school, obtain any instruction, and that instruction which they do receive is of a very imperfect kind." He

---

[1] The first return received was published ; " *Report on the Indigenous Education in Futtehpore*, by William Muir, Esq., 1846." The whole of the reports were subsequently abstracted in an able résumé of the proceedings by Mr. R. Thornton, Esq. :—*Memoir of the Statistics of Indigenous Education in the North-Western Provinces*. In this volume will be found copies of the principal despatches, of which we are here obliged to give necessarily but a limited account.

proposed, therefore, at a cost of from two to four lakhs a year, to grant an endowment in land, for the support of a school in every considerable village throughout the country.[1] The Court of Directors, while concurring in the necessity for more extended means of district education, justly objected to endowments in land, as likely to become hereditary and inefficient. Such a system would, indeed, have proved cumbrous and unmanageable; it would probably have tended to perpetuate the drowsiness and errors of the native method, without any effective

[1] The following is a general outline of the proposal :—

"Statistical inquiries, which have now extended over a great part of the country, show that the people are extremely ignorant, and that existing provisions for the education of the rising generation are very defective. On an average, less than 5 per cent. of the youth who are of an age to attend schools, obtain any instruction, and that instruction, which they do receive, is of a very imperfect kind.

"The people are at the same time poor and unable to support schoolmasters by their own unaided efforts. It therefore becomes the duty of the Government to give them such assistance as may be best calculated to draw forth their own exertions.

"The proposed scheme contemplates the endowment of a school in every village of a certain size, the Government giving up its revenue from the land, which constitutes the endowment, on assurance that the zemindars have appropriated the land for the purpose of maintaining a schoolmaster.

"This system is most in consonance with the customs and feelings of the people. The schoolmaster will become a recognised village servant, elected and supported in a manner consonant with the usage of the village community.

"An endowment in land is preferable to a money payment, because it gives greater respectability of station than a pecuniary stipend much exceeding the rent of the land, and because it connects the schoolmaster with the community in a way which renders his services more acceptable to them than if he were the paid servant of the Government."

6

provision for the prospective introduction of enlightenment and energy; and it could only have been the
strong attachment of Thomason to the "Village
Communities" of the North-West, that led him to
its advocacy.

In 1848, the Lieut.-Governor, taking advantage
of the Honourable Court's expressed willingness to
afford assistance, submitted another plan, in which
endowments, either of land or money, were abandoned, and a system for stimulating indigenous
schools by "advice, assistance, encouragement, and
example," was substituted. Before the close of the
year, the sanction of the Court was received to his
experimental proposal (supported by the Governor-
General), that the scheme should be tried in a circle
of eight districts around Agra, at a yearly expense
of Rs. 50,000. The principles of the measure will
best be understood from the following extract of
orders issued on the 9th of February 1850 :—

RESOLUTION.

"Inquiries, which have been lately instituted in order to ascertain
the state of education throughout these provinces, show that the
greatest ignorance prevails amongst the people, and that there are no
adequate means at work for affording them instruction. The means
of learning are scanty, and the instruction which is given is of the
rudest and least practical character.

"The present scheme contemplates the employment of an agency,
which shall rouse the people to a sense of the evils resulting from
ignorance, which shall stimulate them to exertions on their own part
to remove this ignorance, which shall furnish them with qualified
teachers and appropriate books, and which shall afford rewards and
encouragement to the most deserving teachers and pupils.

"The means of effecting this object will be sought in that feature of the existing revenue system, which provides for the annual registration of all landed property throughout the country.

"It is well known that the land is minutely divided amongst the people. There are few of the agricultural classes who are not possessed of some rights of property in the soil. In order to explain and protect these rights, a system of registration has been devised, which is based on the survey, made at the time of settlement, and which annually shows the state of the property. It is necessary for the correctness of this register, that those, whose rights it records, should be able to consult it and to ascertain the nature of the entries affecting themselves. This involves a knowledge of reading and writing, of the simple rules of arithmetic, and of land measurement.

"The means are thus afforded for setting before the people the practical bearing of learning on the safety of those rights in land, which they most highly prize ; and it is hoped that when the powers of the mind have once been excited into action, the pupils may often be induced to advance further, and to persevere till they reach a higher state of intellectual cultivation.

"The agency by which it is hoped to effect this purpose will be thus constituted.

"There will be a Government village school at the headquarters of every Tehseeldar. In every two or more Tehseeldaris there will be a Pergunnah Visitor. Over these a Zillah Visitor in each district, and over all a Visitor General for the whole of the provinces.

"The Government village school at each Tehseeldari will be conducted by a schoolmaster, who will receive from Government a salary of from ten to twenty rupees per mensem, besides such fees as he may collect from his scholars. The course of instruction in this school will consist of reading and writing the vernacular languages, both Urdu and Hindi, accounts and the mensuration of land according to the native system. To these will be added such instruction in geography, history, geometry, or other general subjects, conveyed through the medium of the vernacular language, as the people may be willing to receive. Care will be taken to prevent these schools from becoming rivals of the indigenous schools maintained by the Natives themselves. This will be effected by making the terms of admission higher than are usually demanded in village schools, and by allowing free admissions only on recommendations given by village schoolmasters, who may be on the Visitor's lists.

. "The Pergunnah Visitors will receive salaries varying from twenty to forty rupees a month. It will be their duty to visit all the towns and principal villages in their jurisdictions, and to ascertain what means of instruction are available to the people. Where there is no village school, they will explain to the people the advantages that would result from the institution of a school ; they will offer their assistance in finding a qualified teacher, and in providing books, etc. Where schools are found in existence, they will ascertain the nature of the instruction and the number of scholars, and they will offer their assistance to the person conducting the school. If this offer is accepted, the school will be entered on their lists, the boys will be examined, and the more advanced scholars noted, improvements in the course or mode of instruction will be recommended, and such books as may be required will be procured. Prizes will be proposed for the most deserving of the teachers or scholars, and the power of granting free admissions to the Tehseeldari school be recorded.

. . . .

" It will be observed that this scheme contemplates drawing forth the energies of the people for their own improvement, rather than actually supplying to them the means of instruction at the cost of the Government. Persuasion, assistance, and encouragement are the means to be principally employed. The greatest consideration is to be shown for the feelings and prejudices of the people, and no interference is ever to be exercised, where it is not desired by those who conduct the institution. The success of the scheme will chiefly appear in the number and character of the indigenous schools, which may be established. The poor may be persuaded to combine for the support of a teacher ; the rich may be encouraged to support schools for their poorer neighbours, and all the schools that are established may be assisted, improved, and brought forward.

" These operations must be conducted in concert with the revenue authorities, and must obtain their cordial assistance. The agency which is now called into action may be made most valuable in ensuring the proper training of putwarris, and in ascertaining the qualifications of candidates or nominees for that office. Certificates of qualification from some of the persons employed in the department may be made necessary for advancement to the post of village putwarri and also to many other appointments, such as those of peon, chupprassi or burkundauze, as well as to those higher offices, where literary attainments are more evidently essential."

Thus, while the scheme aims at encouraging the people to multiply their own schools, it provides in every small division one *Tehseelie* school, as an example of right teaching and a nursery of good teachers, and it brings to bear upon the Native institutions a machinery which, by imparting advice, supervision, and good school-books, will tend to their gradual improvement and elevation. These efforts have been welcomed by the people; for the great value of the plan is that it makes them *work with* us for their own improvement. It is *their own* schools that we are, with their own consent, endeavouring to raise. Hence it is that they willingly receive our teachers, cheerfully accept our suggestions and assistance, and purchase with avidity the useful school-books, which are being prepared with a laborious devotion by Mr. Henry Stewart Reid and his subordinates, and are brought, by the arrangements of the Government, to the very doors of the purchasers. Instead, therefore, of planting amongst them foreign schools, uncongenial to their tastes, and the object of an unconquerable prejudice, —schools that would never take root or germinate in the rare vicinities in which our funds would enable us to open them,—we bring to the cause a legion of assisting Seminaries in every quarter of the land; and, almost unconsciously to themselves, bear along the Nation in the march of intellect, and raise them in the scale of moral life.

The actual result has proved to be no less satisfactory than the anticipation. Although, at so early a period it is hardly fair to expect any sensible effect in a measure, which to affect the large masses of the country must necessarily work with a slow and permeating influence, yet a marked advance has

already been made, as the returns noted below from
Mr. Reid's carefully prepared tables will prove.[1]
While the numbers have materially increased, the
quality of the instruction has greatly improved, and
inflated Persian and rude illiterate Hindi are being

	Schools.	Scholars.
[1] 1850 (probably imperfect) . .	2014	17,169
1850–51	3127	28,636
1851–52	3329	31,843
1852–53	3469	36,884

Dr. Mouat, an impartial and most capable witness, has reported in
terms of unqualified praise regarding the system. Of the examination
of the school at Allyghur, where "some hundreds" of pupils were
collected by Mr. Reid from the district for inspection, he writes :—

"During my long connection with education in India, and
familiarity with the attainments and appearance of the pupils of all
castes and classes, I never witnessed a more gratifying and interesting
scene."

Of the general system he thus speaks : "It will be at once apparent
that the scheme and manner of working it meet with my entire
approval ; it is no small praise of a great plan of national education,
which has barely completed the third year of its existence, to record
that it has not only fully and fairly attained the object for which it was
designed, as far as its limited trial will admit of, but has actually already
outrun its own means of extension, for want of books and instruments
of a higher order than those now in use. In the second year of its
trial in the experimental districts sanctioned, it has raised the number
of boys receiving a sound elementary education from 17,000 to 30,000,
has thrown into the schools between 30,000 and 40,000 school-books
of a better class than those heretofore in use, and has given such an
impulse to the cause of vernacular education as cannot fail, in a very
few years, to produce the fruits that invariably result from a spread
of knowledge in the right direction."

It has become possible by this system to introduce the literary test
for the lowest servants of Government, contemplated in the last paragraph of the resolution quoted above. This was done in the eight
experimental districts, in the resolution of the 8th June 1852, which
prescribes an examination in reading, writing, and accounts, for
putwarris, burkundauzes, chupprassies, and all the officials of the
Government. This is a proceeding in the right direction for moving
the people and raising the masses from below.

steadily forsaken for our simple Urdu school-books and their invaluable stores of knowledge. The sales of school-books alone would show that a system has at last been discovered, suited to the habits and wishes of the people, and rapidly becoming popular and established among them.

Persuaded by these happy results of the success of his scheme, the Lieut.-Governor, within two months of his death, laid its progress in detail before the Government of India, and solicited sanction to extend it over the whole North-West Provinces, at an annual expenditure of two lakhs of rupees. On a review of the proceedings, the Governor-General,—ever ready cordially to appreciate any measure for the advancement of India, and vigorously carry it into effect,—not only approved the extension of the plan throughout these Provinces, but its introduction also into Bengal and the Punjab. The Resolution in which this is embodied contains the following beautiful and touching tribute to the Founder of a system which " experience has shown to be capable of producing such rich and early fruit " ;—

" And while I cannot refrain," His Lordship writes, " from recording anew in this place my deep regret that the ear which would have heard this welcome sanction given, with so much joy, is now dull in death, I desire at the same time to add the expression of my feeling, that even though Mr. Thomason had left no other memorial of his public life behind him, this system of general Vernacular education, which is all his own, would have sufficed to build up for him a noble and abiding monument of his earthly career."

So high a testimony, from such a quarter, renders unnecessary any further eulogium of the scheme from the Reviewer's pen.

Here we close our review of Thomason's official character. It may well be inquired what secret charm it was, which lent to almost every department of his administration so distinguishing an efficiency and greatness. It was not brilliant genius; for his faculties, though powerful and elevated, were not transcendent; it was not the gift of eloquence; nor anything unusually persuasive either in speech or writing. The capacities of his well-regulated mind, schooled into their utmost efficiency, performed wonderful things; but those capacities in themselves were in few respects greater than are often met with in undistinguished characters. There was indeed a rare power of deliberation and judgment, an unusual faculty of discernment and research, a keen discrimination of truth from error. Yet these were mainly the result of studious habit, and earnest purpose. And herein, in our judgment, lies the grand praise of the late administration. It was by LABOUR that it was perfected—conscientious, unceasing, daily labour; by a wakeful anxiety that knew no respite; by a severity of thought, ever busy and ever prolific in the devising of new arrangements, and the perfecting of old. Yet his mind was so beautifully balanced that this unwearied work and never - ceasing tension produced (as in most men it could hardly fail to have done) no irregularity of action, and no fretful or impatient advance. All was even, serene, powerful.

Sternly as Thomason held, in his position of Lieut.-Governor, to the axiom, that the introduction of religious teaching by the Government was not only inexpedient but unjustifiable,[1] he could yet see, as the goal of his measures, both Collegiate and Indigenous, the eventful conversion of the people to Christianity. Scrupulous to the last degree in his official measures, he yet never feared to avow this desire and persuasion privately, and even sometimes, in an unoffensive form, at the public examinations of the Government Colleges. At the latter he has been heard to say, that although bound in his official position to provide seminaries where no reference was made to Christianity, yet in a private capacity, his influence, his money, and his efforts were directed towards imparting elsewhere another element in education, essential to the

[1] He declined to admit the books of the Calcutta Christian School Book Society into the Depôt of the Curator of Government School Books, or to allow the Government shops and colporteurs to exhibit religious works along with their stock of school-books, lest he should prove to be holding out false colours ; enticing the people by the profession of strict religious neutrality, while in reality favouring Christianity at the expense of other religions. If some may not be able entirely to sympathise with this rigid justice, let them remember that it only adds lustre to the public avowals in favour of Christianity, which, in consistence with his principles, he did make, and enhances the value of his private efforts.

well-being and highest interests of the people.[1] The
following extract from his speech at the opening of
the Benares College sufficiently establishes his views
in this respect :—

"We are here met together this day, men of different races and of
different creeds. If any one section of this assembly had met to
dedicate such a building as this to the education of their young in
their own peculiar tenets, they would have given a religious sanction
to the act, and would have consecrated the deed by the ceremonial of
their faith. But this we cannot do. Unhappily, human opinions,
on the subject of religion, are so irreconcilable, that we cannot concur
in any one act of worship. The more necessary it is, then, that each
man, in his own breast, should offer up his prayer to the God whom
he worships,[2] that here morality may be rightly taught, and that here
truth, in all its majesty, may prevail. This aspiration may have a
different meaning, according to the wishes or belief of the person who
forms it ; but with many it will point to a new state of things, when
a higher Philosophy and a purer Faith will pervade this land, not
enforced by the arbitrary decrees of a persecuting government, not
hypocritically professed to meet the wishes of a proselytising government, but, whilst the Government is just and impartial, cordially
adopted by a willing people, yielding to the irresistible arguments
placed before them. Nor is it unreasonable to expect that such a

---

[1] Such, for example, were the sentiments expressed at an examination of the Agra College, when a kindly reference was made to the
new Missionary College just established there.

[2] This phrase has occasioned misapprehension in some quarters, as
if Mr. Thomason had conceded to his idolatrous audience, that the
various gods they worshipped were really the hearers of prayer.
Whatever interpretation the words are capable of, it is certain that
they were simply used with reference to the aspiration which the
speaker desired that all, then present, not excluding the Hindus and
Mohammedans, should raise to the Great Being, whom, one and all, by
an intuitive perception of the heart, feel to be supreme, should pray
that He would bless the institution, and render it an instrument for
His own glory and man's good.

After the criticisms appeared, Mr. Thomason was known to have
expressed much regret that he had not framed the expression in a
manner incapable of misconstruction. But the criticisms were in
themselves hypercritical.

change may take place. We cannot forget that to such a change we owe the present happy state of things in our own country ; and, even in this country, changes of the same nature have taken place. It is but a few days ago that our friend, Major Kittoe, who is as distinguished for antiquarian research as he is for the architectural skill he has shown in this edifice, led a party to view the neighbouring ruins around Sárnáth. He there showed us the undoubted remains of another and a different system which once prevailed in this land. He showed us its temples, its colleges, its hospitals, and its tombs, now perished and long buried under the earth. A few centuries have so utterly destroyed it, that it is now only known in this part of the country, from the obscure allusions of Chinese travellers, the scarcely legible inscriptions on broken sculptures, and the imperfect traditions of a despised sect. And now there flourishes here, on the banks of the Ganges, another system, still vigorous, but already on the wane. And that system may pass away, and give place to Another and a Better one. From this place may this system spread throughout ; nor is it vain to hope that the building in which we are assembled may be one instrument in the mighty change. When it is so, the highest aspirations of those who first designed and mainly promoted its erection will be fully realised.

" Such is the assured hope and expectation of many here assembled, and there is a large section of the remainder who share in the expectation, but cannot bring themselves at present to adopt it as their hope. But no undue means will here be employed to effect the end. No religious system will here be exclusively taught. This is a common arena, on which all can assemble, and where the common element of truth can be impartially acquired. Let all to whom the cause of Truth is sacred, co-operate in promoting the objects of this building. To withdraw from the field will but show that they are conscious of the weakness of their cause."

Beyond the mere social and intellectual elevation, anticipated from his system of indigenous Village education, Thomason believed that it was the truest foundation on which to build our efforts for the spiritual regeneration of the country.[1] Sound and

[1] One great beauty of the system is its power of development and adaptation to the advancing circumstances of the country. It would adjust itself as readily (which the land endowment would not have done) to a Christianised tract of villages, as it now does to the most

enlightened secular tuition is, indeed, the most substantial fulcrum upon which the Christian lever can be brought to work ; and the most enlightened of our Missionaries concur in holding the improved Village schools to be the pioneers of their own labours.

Of Missionary institutions he was the warm advocate, the ready helper,[1] and the munificent patron. Every evangelical denomination scattered throughout the Provinces received his substantial assistance; although, wherever a Mission of his own Church existed, he considered it to be entitled to his peculiar if not exclusive assistance. His charity was not, however, confined to missionary objects :—no case of benevolence, no cry of real distress, nor any public endeavour for the Social welfare within the length and breadth of the North-West Provinces, if well supported (for he was discriminating in his charity), missed his liberal aid. Colleges, schools, dispensaries, churches, charities—whatever in fact tended to ameliorate or to elevate the social life of the people, either native or European, was liberally aided. His

bigoted and intolerant Hindu and Mohammedan ones. Christian and Missionary schools share Mr. H. S. Reid's favours equally with Village indigenous ones. The scheme is in fact an aid to *all spontaneous effort* which has secular education for one of its main objects ; and thus it resembles the solution of the educational difficulty now recognised in England.

[1] At a former period he afforded personal aid to their labours, by preparing a revised translation of the Psalms. The version is still in use. It is distinguished by its elegance, but the style is too high and difficult for the comprehension of the mass of the people.

almsgiving eminently responded (wherever that was possible) to the direction of being done in secret. None but his chosen almoners knew of some of his most liberal and spontaneous acts; and wherever publicity was unavoidable, the courteous modesty of the donor only enhanced the value of the gift. A tenth portion of his income was carefully appropriated to *bonâ fide* charities; but the largeness of the heart, and the depth of his sympathy for debased and suffering humanity, were ever prompting him to overleap the limit; and, notwithstanding the large scale of his income, and his inexpensive habits, he died (and in his last hours felt it to be a satisfaction that he was dying) a man of small fortune.

A certain amount of outward dignity, he believed that his position called for; and (looking upon his high allowances as fixed by this consideration) he made a point of conscience to maintain it. But the love of display found no place in his heart: pomp and show he regarded with indifference, and he was markedly distinguished by an unostentatious bearing. Though given to no false self-depreciation, and holding that manly front which a just self-respect requires, still his humility and modesty were conspicuous in every action. A serene and cheerful benevolence ever beamed from his countenance; his frame was spare, and his figure unusually tall, slightly stooped, but his carriage was nevertheless eminently suited to the nobility of his mind; and his features (not perhaps in themselves striking) were so lighted up with intellect and benignity as to win the most casual stranger, and diffuse light and love amongst his immediate circle. His temperament was naturally cold, his manner distant, and his demeanour constrained; still such was the force of the counter-elements, that warmth, ease, and kindness were the prevailing characteristics, which even a short acquaintance would discover. His temper was calm and unruffled by provocation. Though the bent of his mind was to follow out favourite principles to an extreme (some perhaps thought an unjustifiable) limit, he was yet singularly tolerant of difference of opinion where no axiom of morality was involved; and views the most discordant with his own were always heard with kindness, and combated patiently, but with a wonderful fertility of argument. His religious sentiments were pure from the modern and prevalent tincture of Pharisaism, and " in strict accordance with the large and scriptural views of the blessed Reformers and Martyrs of our Church ";[1] still, with a moderation rare in our day, he cherished, esteemed, and loved the good of every Denomination, even where the most extreme and opposing principles were strenuously held. His feelings were always under a stern command, and he would to a very careful looker-on appear unmoved and unconcerned, at times when the most lively and

[1] Sermon preached by the Venerable Archdeacon Pratt, at the Cathedral, Calcutta, on the 16th October 1853. This Sermon contained some passages powerfully descriptive of Thomason's character; a personal intimacy enabling the preacher to draw from the life.

intense emotions were busy within his breast. In private friendships, his attachments were steady, unselfish, unreserved; but a common faith added a peculiar depth and strength to the bond. His domestic affections were amongst the strongest and most pervading that we have ever witnessed; and if we could tear away the curtain from the delicacy of private life, the exquisite tenderness of a father's love would add the brightest touch to the portraiture of a character the most perfect and the most attractive it has been our lot to know. Duty, sincerity, love, were the watchwords of his life; the one idea which formed his spring of action—THE GOOD OF OTHERS.

And the key to all this was a Christian faith. He believed the Bible to be the Word of God; and therefore took it for the daily and the hourly guide of his life. A simple faith in Christ, as his Divine Redeemer, was followed by an unquestioning devotion to His service. Hence followed love to men, and earnest endeavour for their welfare. These motive powers (concealed it may be from the outward observer) were deeply seated in his soul, and imparted a consistent and energetic action to the whole machinery of his life. However engrossing the claims of the State, those of his God were paramount: and it was just by a daily subjection of heart to the principles of the Gospel, and by honouring supremely the claims of his Maker, that he was enabled so efficiently to discharge his duty toward his earthly Master and his Sovereign.

We quote (from the Sermon noticed at the head of this review) the following account of Mr. Thomason's Christian life by the Rev. T. V. French,[1] with the more pleasure, because, while eminently qualified to form a judgment, the independent position and devoted life of the Preacher place his opinion beyond the suspicion of any partial influence :—

"In such a sense we believe the words of our text[2] were specially appropriate to him who is gone from us. His public character can only enter into our consideration here, so far as it was influenced by his private character as a Christian. The influence which this exercised was uniform, and pervaded his whole course of action. There are few who would not bear witness readily to the simplicity and singleness of heart with which he set God's glory before him, as the steady and undeviating object of his life. From the conscientious discharge of his duties to the State, he never separated the sense of accountability to One higher than the State : not acting as though there were two masters to be served, two rules of action, two principles of guidance to be followed, two irreconcilable duties to be performed. Rather acknowledging but one source and fountainhead of duty, beside which, and apart from which, there could be no outgoings of it ; it was his study, while having regard to the lesser aspects in which subjects might be viewed, to view them not the less in their religious bearing, and to trace them up to their connection with the highest of all duties. Doubtless the great secret of this line of conduct may be found here ; that he was accustomed, in every important and difficult matter, to have recourse to God in prayer for direction and guidance. With a mind thus composed, and as before God, arriving at a decision, he had the strongest ground of assurance which man can have, that his work would be prospered and rewarded : that confidence which produces steadiness of action, firmness of purpose, and can patiently abide difficulties and delays. Very edifying it was to observe the guardedness with which he walked ; and the fear which he expressed, lest the incessant calls of duty should check the growth of spiritual life in his soul. In the enlargement of Christ's kingdom, and making

---

[1] Afterwards Bishop of Lahore.

[2] "From henceforth let no man trouble me, for I bear in my body the marks of the Lord Jesus" ; 17th verse of Galatians vi., a chapter which the dying statesman desired to be read in his hearing.

known His pure and saving truth to the heathen around us, he always expressed a lively and heartfelt interest, which he extended even to the individual cases and circumstances of any in whose heart a desire had been awakened for the reception of Christianity. He seemed fully persuaded of the happy and blessed effects which would be wrought on the Hindu mind and character by embracing our Holy Faith. I have a vivid impression left on my own mind of the bright and animated expression of countenance with which he detailed to me, some months ago, the circumstances of two important conversions which had taken place in Delhi : tidings of which he had just received. Having watched patiently and attentively the course of Christian missions, and par- taken much in the hopes and fears which they have alternately awakened, he was sensibly affected with the report of anything which seemed to make against the progress of the truth : was fully alive to difficulties : would suggest new plans ; and point to fresh directions in which the Christian effort of each labourer engaged in the work might extend itself. One of those brought up in the Orphan Institu- tion at Secundra was most touchingly describing to me (since the tidings of his death were received) how he would, in bygone years, · come over to the Mission premises there, gather the children around him, and, seating himself in the middle of them, would question them in the simple Bible Histories they had prepared, and spend much pains in the explanation of them ; so that his visits were always welcomed and talked of amongst them. He would speak feelingly of the state of the native servants in his employ, and of the earnest desire he had to bring them within reach of direct Christian in- struction.

"The strength of his religious convictions was not independent of a mature consideration of all the main difficulties that were urged against the Christian religion. He spoke as one who had seriously reflected upon them : allowed them all their due weight : but found that pre- ponderating evidence in support of the faith once delivered to the Saints, which led him, with advancing years, to glory increasingly in bearing about with him the marks of the Lord Jesus.

"In us, who were strengthened and encouraged by observing those marks, I believe the remembrance of him will live, and will not readily be effaced. Many a distressed and afflicted one can bear witness to the timely help he rendered, often unsolicited, and even diligently seeking out the objects of it, unknown to any but his Father who '*seeth in secret*.' His unassuming, reverent, prayerful demeanour, which was a blessed example to us in the House of prayer of which he was so regular an attendant, helping to quicken us in our devotions, involuntarily reproving the wandering eye and heart in those who were

7

his fellow-worshippers ; [1] the remembrance of serious counsel suggested as occasion offered ; the recollection of an influence calmly and uniformly exerted over those amongst whom he went in and out, to their spiritual and temporal good :—these are hallowed memorials, which will stay with us, I believe, and recall to us the image of one, who was as a ruler, that which he was as a man ; one whom Christian principles swayed to Christian practice."

Such is the man (and it is one of the hopeful symptoms of our age) whom the public has united to honour. Witness after witness has borne testimony before the Legislature of Britain, to the pre-eminent virtues of his Administration : the Press has conspired to denominate his, "the model Government." The praises of the Honourable Court, and of the Governor-General under whom he acted, have been freely and frequently accorded. And when at last the State was deprived by death of its able servant, an *Extra-ordinary Gazette*, encircled by the ensigns of mourning, announced the fact to India :—

"FORT WILLIAM—HOME DEPARTMENT.

"*The 3rd October* 1853.

"NOTIFICATION.—The Most Noble the Governor-General of India in Council is deeply grieved to announce the decease of the Honourable James Thomason, the Lieut.-Governor of the North-Western Provinces.

---

[1] Most Civil Officers in the North-Western Provinces will long remember how, on the appointed weekly halt (for he always prized and carefully observed the Sunday, wholly casting aside the cares of State, substituting the records of Christianity for the weary files of official labour, and devoting himself to his family and the special duties of the day), the bell of the Camp would sound forth an invitation to the public tent, where, in a manner impressive and earnest, the service of the Church was performed by the Lieut.-Governor himself.

"The Lieut.-Governor has long since earned for himself a name, which ranks him high among the most distinguished servants of the Honourable East Indian Company.

"Conspicuous ability, devotion to the public service, and a conscientious discharge of every duty, have marked each step of his honourable course : while his surpassing administrative capacity, his extensive knowledge of affairs, his clear judgment, his benevolence of character and suavity of demeanour, have adorned and exalted the high position which he was wisely selected to fill.

"The Governor-General in Council deplores his loss with a sorrow deep and unfeigned,—with sorrow aggravated by the regret that his career should have thus been untimely closed, when all had hoped that opportunities for extended usefulness were still before him, and that fresh honour might be added to his name.

"The Most Noble the Governor-General in Council directs that the Flag shall be lowered half-mast high, and that seventeen minute guns [1] shall be fired at the respective seats of Government in India so soon as the present Notification shall have been there received.

"By order of the Governor-General of India in Council.

"GEO. PLOWDEN,

"*Offg. Secy. to the Govt. of India.*"

The Governor-General has also, in terms most gratifying to the friends of the deceased statesman, proposed to the Court of Directors to found at the Roorkee College (which, the object of his fostering care during life, may well perpetuate his name after death), a Scholarship commemorative of the ability

[1] It has been said in some quarters that minute guns corresponding in number with the age of the deceased should have been fired : but this is a mistake. At the funeral of Military and Civil Officers, the minute guns are strictly limited, by Royal Warrant, to the number the deceased was entitled to as a salute. The Governor-General paid a peculiar tribute to the memory of the Lieut.-Governor, in directing this honour to be shown at each of the seats of Government.

and virtues of Mr. Thomason. All honour to the Most Noble Marquess, for the just and generous praise he has so freely accorded. It will not be viewed as one of the least of the praises of his administration, thus to have appreciated, and honourably acknowledged, the merits of one who rendered such distinguished service to his Government.

So high indeed was the estimate of the Governor-General, that we believe he had pressed upon the Government of Britain and the Court of Directors the appointment of Thomason, as the fittest man, to the Government of Madras. And it is a singular confirmation of the wisdom of the advice, that before it could have been received at home, the appointment so recommended had been actually made. Thus did Thomason retire from this earthly scene, honoured in death as in life, by his Noble Master, by the Honourable Court, and by the Government of his native land.

And if, as we believe from Holy Writ, the spirits of just men made perfect are inheritors of "glory, honour, and immortality," may we not anticipate that a nobler work, and a more enviable recompense than that of an earthly Sovereign, await him at another and a sublimer Court? Thither, trusting to his Saviour's merits, he dared with confidence to approach; for he was heard at the last to say, that though unworthy and deficient, "*he was not afraid to die.*" And there, we cannot doubt, with nobler faculties, and an inconceivably vaster sphere of action, he but continues the service of that Great Master, for whom, upon earth, he delighted to labour, and rejoices in a glory and a reward before which his terrestrial distinctions, like the minor luminaries at the Sun's approach, wane and vanish.

PRINTED BY MORRISON AND GIBB LIMITED, EDINBURGH